"GOT SOME FRIENDS WHO WANT TO MEET YOU," SCALZANNI SAID.

Suddenly he struck—swooping both hands and the meathooks in them down like the flapping wings of a condor. They came together like brain-crushing tongs in midair with a sudden eruption of sparks as metal slammed against metal. But Stone was gone, having danced a good yard away. The guy was fast, incredibly fast. He'd have to wait for the little slime to make a mistake.

But it was Stone who made the mistake. He stepped backward and found himself toppling over a root. Then he was lying flat on his back, his knife by his side. Scalzanni charged forward flailing away with both hooks like some sort of psychotic Captain Hook.

The meathook in the Mafia killer's right hand descended like a question mark searching for blood toward Stone's skull . . .

D1737867

ALSO BY CRAIG SARGENT

The Last Ranger
The Savage Stronghold
The Madman's Mansion
The Rabid Brigadier
The War Weapons

**Published by
POPULAR LIBRARY**

THE WARLORD'S REVENGE

CRAIG SARGENT

POPULAR LIBRARY

An Imprint of Warner Books, Inc.

A Warner Communications Company

POPULAR LIBRARY EDITION

Copyright © 1988 by Warner Books, Inc.
All rights reserved.

Popular Library® and the fanciful P design are registered
trademarks of Warner Books, Inc.

Popular Library books are published by
Warner Books, Inc.
666 Fifth Avenue
New York, N.Y. 10103

 A Warner Communications Company

Printed in the United States of America

First Printing: January, 1988

10 9 8 7 6 5 4 3 2 1

Chapter One _____

I f death be a painter, then its murderous brush swept
across the sky in broad, radioactive strokes of blood-red,
pumpkin-orange, and shroud-black with a deft master's
touch. A mushroom cloud, a mosaic of writhing color and
absolute blackness, rose above the prairie lands of northern
Colorado like a tower of cancer. It was as if all the fires of
hell had released their foul smoke at once and these spires of
total disintegration had joined into one great cloud that
loomed above the earth like a monument to the apocalypse.
Up it rose, unstoppable, into the cloud line and beyond, an
immense, hideous sculpture to the folly of mankind.

The mushroom headed straight up ten miles and then
spread out flat at the top, as if it were being sliced off by the
high winds of the upper atmosphere—that part of its radioactivity being swept off to all portions of the world to add a
little more poison to the soil and water. As if the planet earth
hadn't been poisoned enough already. The smell of the
burned dead was just beginning to permeate the countryside,
a scent that would linger for a long time. There were a million tons of steamed blood and molten life to be found in the
dark cloud, in the swirling smoke that was but the remnants
of the atomic fury that had erupted just minutes before.

The skies around the black pillar—which had the appearance of an immense tornado now, its four-mile-wide funnel
swirling slowly like the gas storms of Jupiter—were a vi-
brant purple-and-green color, the color of air before

lightning strikes, the color of a corpse's cheeks. The ghostly glow seemed to suffuse the entire horizon in every direction, and the heavens above. Even the stars, winking down in horror, appeared orange and yellow, tinted like diseased little spots, pimples of rot in the wounded night.

"The air tastes like shit," Martin Stone said, turning toward Meyra, whose eyes were wet and reflective, like little pools of perfect pain. The Indian woman didn't actually cry as much as release a constant stream of salty moisture that flowed from the inner edges of each eye. The tears flowed down, streaming across her cheeks and between her lips as she sucked unconsciously at them.

But then, she had a right to cry, and to continue to cry forever. Her brother, Little Bear, the leader of a small band of Cheyenne, had just been burned to a crisp by the detonation of the ten-meg atomic warhead that had blown its top some thirty miles to the north of them.

Meyra tried not to look, but she couldn't help it and turned again to glance down at what had been her brother. It was horrible. Terribly, revoltingly, vomitingly horrible. It was as if he had just melted. A plastic toy taken by a sadistic child into his playroom and burned with a blowtorch. Turned over and over like an animal on a spit and splayed with the fire until he was no longer human but a melted thing whose features—nose, eyes, lips, and neck—all dripped and blended into one another like an amorphous Jell-o, its teeth poking out here and there from a puddle of flesh at its feet.

Little Bear's skeleton still remained somehow. Sort of. It, too, had been twisted and plied by atomic fingers so it looked like an anatomist's nightmare—ribs curving out at all different angles, some bent in, leg bones broken in numerous places. The whole thing was like something that had been put through a bone crusher, something Picasso might have sculpted to show the horror of war. The true ugliness of death.

Meyra lurched suddenly toward the smoking mess of human debris in quick little steps, and Stone rushed forward as he saw her stumble and start to collapse. Her body hurtled straight toward the bubbling pit of what had once been her brother—only Stone's strong arms reached out at the last second and pulled her back from crashing into the smoking remains. Her eyes were spinning around in her head like Ping-Pong balls, just the whites showing. He half carried her back a few yards and came to one knee, holding her on his leg, cradled in his arms. He could feel her quivering like a terrified animal.

After a few minutes, those who were left of the attack force Martin Stone had assembled gathered around him and Meyra, who remained motionless in his arms. They just stood in a loose circle around the frozen pair, not sure what to say, overwhelmed by the immensity of the atomic blast they had just lived through, and the still rising mushroom cloud, its reds and oranges fading to steel-gray and black as its revolutions per minute, its turning stack of radioactive particles and melted life, also slowed. A cyclone of death, barely moving. But then it had all the time in the world. The hydrogen bomb had gone off quickly—in one ten-millionth of a second. But it was the fallout cloud, the radiation, that would get to enjoy the lingering destruction, frolicking in it for months, as all living things caught in its path slowly became diseased, rotted and died away.

Martin Stone looked up from his own dark thoughts as he suddenly realized they were waiting for him to do something. God knows what. But they had no one else to turn to—just filthy, ashen faces looking, for all their toughness and macho, like little kids who were lost and unutterably alone. Being in the vicinity of a nuke blast can do that to a man sometimes. Put him a little on the melancholy side. The towering black pyre miles to the north seemed to sing out their names on the hot, radioactive breezes, as if the cloud knew it had missed something but would be back to claim it.

"Oh, for chrissake," Stone yelled out angrily as he stared around at the remnants of the bizarre attack force he had managed to assemble to take on General Patton and his Fascist New American Army—four recruits from the NAA itself who had come to join him (there had been eight just twenty-four hours earlier). And seven of the Cheyenne left. Little Bear was dead. Leaderless, the Indians, all of them so stone-faced and tough when he had first encountered them —with their stoic, coppery faces; long black hair, and buckskin jackets—didn't seem nearly so sure of themselves now. Even they looked toward Stone with odd expressions. What the hell did they expect him to—

"Well, at least put some wraps over your faces, assholes," Stone said gruffly as a little wave of black stuff seemed to suddenly float down over them like ashes from the sky. "You breathe this stuff in . . ." He spoke through his own mash of wet fabric that covered his nose and mouth, catching some of the black ash on his palm. It was still hot. Stone released it just as quickly, and it swirled to the blast-strewn ground like a dark feather joining the blanket of debris that had swept across the terrain for nearly fifty miles, covering everything with a dark, gritty sand that was still warm beneath their feet. ". . . and you're dead men, as surely as if that motherfucker over there"—he eyed the cloud, which seemed to grow thicker and darker every minute—"had chewed you up in its fires."

A few of the Cheyenne folded their arms as if to indicate that they were men enough to breathe in any goddamn thing they felt like breathing. But the rest of the men, Indians and raw NAA recruits alike, found strips of cloth here and there among their packs on the backs of their three-wheeled bikes that stood parked in a rough circle some thirty yards off. They wet the strips down with water from their gourds and canteens and tied them securely around the lower portions of their faces, so that all the air coming in through their noses and mouths was being crudely, if fairly efficiently, filtered. Stone knew that once the bomb blast was past, it was the particles floating around in the air that were the most danger. Breathing them in, getting them lodged in lung tissue, could mean disease, cancer, months or even years later. The promise of radioactivity was that it never stopped radiating; it would still be glowing long after the remains of the body it had inhabited—and destroyed—was melted back into indecipherable dirt.

Within minutes they were reassembled around Stone with their makeshift gas masks on, their eyes now staring at him with even more desperation than before, more pleading, without daring to plead. Stone knew why he had been so dubious of this "leader" role. He had been pretty much on his own—until now. And that he could deal with. If he died? Well, there wouldn't be a hell of a lot tears to mourn him. But with men under his command—with all that entailed—he'd have to change careers fast. He couldn't explain to them why. Couldn't give them the slightest comfort at the edges of hell. He couldn't even answer those questions himself. Why had it all happened? Why had America collapsed into barbarism and savagery? Why did crime lords and murderers rule the once great country that was nothing now but a thousand little principalities, a thousand little sadistic dictators and princes of death? Why had men reverted to cannibalism, sacrifice? Why had his own mother been . . . No, these were questions he didn't even ask himself. What fucking right had this bunch to look at him like that?

"And what about you two?" Stone asked as he stood up and looked at the two Cheyenne who remained maskless, smirking at the rest of their band. Meyra turned away from the group as she dabbed at her eyes, not wanting the others to see her with tears. It was not befitting an Indian to show pain. Especially not one with the blood of Cheyenne royalty in her veins. Their culture had evolved for thousands of years, the rule being to swallow pain. But it wasn't her brother's death that disturbed her so but that she had seen him in that state—that repose of wretched decay. He was like a beacon of horror, a black lamp that kept pulling her eyes toward it. Like looking down at a mortal wound in one's own chest that meant annihilation. Meyra could not tear her eyes away from the charred corpse some twelve yards off, kneeling as if in prayer in the center of the oily brown-and-black puddle that was its melted flesh and organs, forming a rough circle for about a yard around it. An Indian Buddha in death meditation.

"Don't need to," snarled back one of the two Cheyenne who still had his face unmasked, the taller and nastier-looking one. "White men need that sort of protection. But not us." He slapped himself on the chest, and then so did his shorter friend, who looked around at the other Indians with a shit-eating grin.

"Suit yourself, pal," Stone replied coolly. "But don't come running to me when your nose starts running red and you cough and a river comes out. 'Cause there won't be nothing I can do."

"Didn't ask you to do nothing," the Indian said, holding up a turquoise amulet. "Cheyenne medicine is all I need, man. White medicine causes cancer." The Cheyenne was a few inches taller than Stone, though very lean and lanky like a snake. His lower lip was all busted, an injury from long ago. It had healed over completely but made him seem to have lost a portion of his mouth, the lip having been reduced to the size of a pencil line, a light purplish color. It gave him an oddly buck-toothed appearance on the upper right portion of his face, as his teeth tended to poke out all the way to the roots like the partial grin of a skull.

He sneered at Stone and opened his mouth and his arms to the sky, taking in deep breaths of the foul ash that was starting to fall a little thicker now, in long sheets, misty and ephemeral, floating down almost gracefully and spinning around like black snowflakes. The dark ash was sucked into the Indian's mouth and lungs before he realized the particles were burning him, scalding his tongue and throat. He exploded out in a violent cough, and the others could see the little red marks where the hot ash had made contact with the membranes of his mouth.

The Cheyenne smiled proudly at the Indians, who seemed impressed by his "bravery" but deigned to keep their flimsy shields of cloth over their fallout-coated faces. Bravery was one thing, being an asshole was something else.

"We've got to bury him," Meyra said suddenly, loudly, and firmly, startling Stone from his eye-to-eye with the still coughing Cheyenne—Leaping Elk, if Stone remembered correctly. The Indian had been second-in-command of the small band of nomads. Little Bear had easily fended off his halfhearted attempts at rule. But now... Already Leaping Elk was trying to take command of the remaining Cheyenne braves through feats of daring, an almost mad kind of Indian courage with a contempt for death. Already he was going to challenge Stone for leadership of the hybrid fighting force. But for the moment, anyway, the others didn't seem like they were too interested in sucking in radioactive fallout.

Stone made a mental note to keep an eye on the macho Cheyenne. There was something crazy in those eyes that he didn't like at all.

"What?" Stone asked, turning to Meyra, who stared at him, her eyes hardly able to focus on his face. Her lips were white, her deeply tanned skin looked almost pale in her state of near emotional breakdown. Yet even now Martin Stone found it hard not to see her beauty, the perfect ridges and curves of her young face. And found it hard not to remember lying hard against the perfect young body that had pressed back against him with animal desire. Stone suddenly felt a sharp headache sweep through his head, whether from the radiation they had all doubtless absorbed or because of the sudden twinge of guilt he felt over memories of fucking her when she was staring at her barbecued brother, who was sending out foul-smelling smoke signals that he had been overcooked.

"I said we've got to bury him," Meyra repeated in a kind of gasping hiss, as if she couldn't quite find the air to talk. She, too, wore one of the masks, and it made it hard to suck in what little oxygen there was out there.

"But—" Stone began to protest as gently as he could, as he stared over at the bubbling garbage dump of a man, knowing that it would be impossible to bury it; it would come apart in their hands. The still boiling flesh of the brain and the bubbling organs occasionally burped up steam in the center of what had been the stomach, kidneys, liver, intestines, all melted down into a thick black stew as dense as oil and which glowed with an infinitesimal blue flame along its entire surface.

"No, Martin Stone, do not argue with me," the Cheyenne fighting woman replied coldly. "He *must* be buried. It is the Cheyenne way. For a warrior of my people to die in battle and not be buried according to our most sacred rituals is what you call blasphemy. You understand, Stone. His soul would rot in a limbo of death rather than be reborn into a world of peace and a plenitude of animals. We would condemn him to the Cheyenne version of eternal damnation. If a people do not even bury their dead but leave them to lie out and be consumed by the coyotes, the lizards, that people deserves to die."

"All right, all right," Stone said softly, holding his hands up as if to ward her off. "You win. But we'd better hurry." He squinted, taking in the movement of the great swirling cloud. It still didn't seem to be in a hurry to get to them. Just expanding out from the middle like a tire being pumped with air. The wind currents tonight, thank God, were minimal.

The other Cheyenne had just grunted out general noises of assent as Meyra had spoken, but as Stone started toward the radiation-cooked flesh, not one of them made a move to help him. Stone felt his guts tighten up, as if they might release whatever was still down in there from the day before. He looked slowly down at the remains of the man he had come to know and respect. There weren't many men around anymore who were basically decent—and tough enough to back it up. That made the hideousness of the Cheyenne chief's remains that much more terrible.

Stone circled around the human bonfire, tightening the bandanna around his mouth and nose. The smell of the cauldron of steaming organs in the center of the black-ash pelvic bone was repulsive. He had smelled burning flesh before—cannibalism was not all that unusual these days. But this was far worse somehow, sweeter—with a burning chemical edge of spiciness. He kept circling, trying to figure out a way to move the smoking thing. There wasn't any. It wasn't even a solid thing—or even a *few* solid things. The bottom of it was just puddle, with fingernails, teeth, and bones of fingers and toes all half submerged like prehistoric fossils beneath the surface. The flame-rippling hulk resting in the center was an uneven mesh of bone and charred, leathery skin that still crisscrossed the inner skeleton like dark webs. Somehow the skull had stayed atop the black ribs, but it was tilted sideways at an angle of nearly ninety degrees, hanging on by the tail of the medulla oblongata, which had hardened from the flames into a leathery tendril that rose from the top of the flaming spinal cord and into the skull. The bubbling brain inside stewed away, as if trying to get ready in time for dinner.

Stone glanced up and over at Meyra, who was staring across at him, her whole body still shaking, he could see, even from ten yards off. She wasn't going to come and help. That was for damn sure. Two of the Cheyenne stepped forward at last, seeing that they must help their fallen leader. Stone couldn't recognize them for sure beneath their breathing bandannas, but he thought one of them was Fighting Eagle, whom Little Bear had mentioned as wanting to be his eventual successor.

"Got to dig hole first," the brave said, walking a few feet to his parked cross-country bike and extracting a folding shovel from a backpack. "I'll dig it right next to his body so we can just push it in. This whole thing doesn't have to be all beautiful, you know, for the ritual to be fulfilled." Stone thought he caught a slightly cynical wink from above the mask. He was sure they hadn't stopped to bury all their dead before. When you're attacked, you try to survive. That's the oldest ritual.

After a few minutes of digging in the loose dirt of the sun-parched backland, the Cheyenne had made a hole about a foot and a half deep, two feet wide, and about six feet long. He stepped back, looked down with vague approval, and handed the shovel to Stone, who started to protest.

"Man who lead man to his death—that man must bury him. Cheyenne words. Cheyenne law. Understand?" Stone felt like he was being pushed to the limits of his own cool, but he couldn't break. He *had* led them all here. Even though the reason for doing so had been imperative, still he was responsible for the deaths. It was true.

Chastened, Stone gritted his teeth and stood above the yard or so of smoking human garbage. He tried to wedge the shovel in beneath the V-shaped pelvic bone, above which the rest of the ashy body rested precariously, but the moment that metal touched bone, the bone crumbled into a hundred little pieces. Inside the glowing hulk he could see the red coals still throbbing peacefully, like the burned-down coals of a long-flaming log. There was no way he was going to transport the thing with any kind of dignity—he could see that right away. Well, he would bury the guy, Stone thought

without looking around at the others, but it wasn't going to
win the Funeral of the Month Award.

He heard a sharp intake of breath from behind him as he
dug the shovel into the pile of collapsed bones and flaming
slime and lifted a bunch of it like mud from the ground. He
threw the load a few feet or so down into the grave, where it
sizzled against the slight wetness from below. Again he dug
the shovel in, this time getting most of the burning mass
onto its curved metal plate. The smell of the charred flesh
was intense for a second and burned Stone's eyes as a sudden breeze fanned the corpse chops right into his face. But
he threw the load forward, and it spread apart as it tumbled
into the grave, steaming as it touched moisture.

The bones and the chunks of burning flesh were the easy
part. It was the actual puddle that was going to be hard. The
stuff was more like boiling tar or oil than something that had
been human. After a few feeble attempts at loading the
wretched waste onto the shovel, Stone just turned the blade
of the implement on its edge and swept it all sideways. The
sticky mess flowed along the ground, pouring down into the
grave to join its more solid brethren parts. Within a couple
of minutes Stone had scraped all that he could of the recently
deceased into the hole. Just a black scum remained on the
ground where Little Bear had died.

Meyra walked over to the stuff in the hole and took her
amulet from around her neck. A beautiful necklace of violet
turquoise adorned with cougar teeth, it created the shape of a
mountain lion, her family crest. The Cheyenne woman
threw it down into the bubbling black mass that had been her
brother, and it was gobbled down in a flash. A thing of
beauty disappeared into a thing of unspeakable horror.

"From this moment on," she said, raising her hands to the
skies overhead, trying to find a patch of clear heaven
through the mists and spreading smoke of the atomic bomb
cloud so she could find and address the ancient Indian Gods,
"from this moment on, I am no one," she said in a hoarse
whisper. "I have no family. I am the last of no lineage. I will
live from minute to minute. I will live only to avenge my

brother. There will be no other life. I will take the place *he* filled in life. I will become him, as he becomes you."

She lowered her eyes to the cauldron of radioactive rot that farted out bursts of pure foulness and took in, without any mental shield, what her brother had become. She wanted to know. Wanted to see the total horror. And remember it for the rest of her life.

Chapter Two _____

"**L**et's get the hell out of here," Stone said none too ceremoniously when Meyra had finished and stood with her head bowed and eyes closed. He didn't know if she was in a religious trance or unconscious, but the mushroom cloud was starting to lean precipitously toward them now, the black curtains of superheated atoms starting to extend out at the very edges like a mist, a dark, blinding fog that crept out over the desolated prairie.

"Don't you bury your dead?" Leaping Elk smirked, his hands on his hips as he stood next to the Bradley III tank, now on its side. Inside the tank were three of Stone's NAA recruits. At least, they had been three of Stone's recruits— mere lads not even out of their teens. Nothing living could have taken the temperature the tank had risen to as it had been caught in the direct radiation and heat waves of the hydrogen bomb. It still seemed to throb an almost invisible violet color, as if it were alive beneath the steel skin.

"That's their coffin," Stone replied icily as he rose and searched for Excaliber, his worse-for-wear bullterrier. "No one, no animal, will get inside that thing for a long, long time. And if they did, they'd be dead before they crawled back out the hatch."

"Why?" Leaping Elk sneered again. "Is it guarded by some invisible white god?" He shot his right hand out and touched the side of the tank—and half screamed, pulling the hand back as it sizzled and burned against the armored steel, which was at a temperature of 1,435 degrees. The others laughed, even his fellow Cheyenne, and Leaping Elk's lips ground furiously against each other. More than anything, he seemed to have the need to be taken seriously, not to be laughed at. His whole face seemed to flush a few shades darker, and with a snorting laugh the Cheyenne stuck his hand back out and this time clamped it down hard against the armor.

Some of the others gasped, and Stone looked away for a second as a stream of smoke went up above the fingers. They could hear the flesh burning beneath the hot metal. But Leaping Elk didn't wince or make a sound. He took in their gaze, basking in their respect—nay, fear—of him, and laughed loud.

After about ten seconds he removed the hand and held it up for all to see. It was literally smoking, the flesh almost black in some places, red and bubbling up like a tar street on a hot summer day in others. The pain seemed to give him pleasure as he grinned, showing the mutilated appendage around. A mark of madness. A mark of the crazy wisdom of the Cheyenne. Stone looked quickly at the eyes of the other braves. And he could see that Leaping Elk's shenanigans were working. Whether he was clever enough to plan it all out or a complete madman, Stone had no idea. But the rest of the Cheyenne were definitely looking at their chortling compatriot with a perverse respect.

"This is what the Cheyenne warrior can do," the brave said, holding the sizzling palm up so that Stone could get a good view.

"And this is what the white man can do," Stone said with a thin grin as he lowered himself down on top of his Harley 1200. "Get his ass the fuck out of here." The bike was beat-up, covered with the grit and grime of warfare. But it felt good beneath his legs as Stone settled down on it, armed to the teeth and ready to fly. He whistled and a low shape appeared out of the dust, shook itself, and leapt up onto the black leather seat behind him.

"Good boy." Stone grinned, scratching the animal behind the ears. A little cloud of dust rose above its head, and the pitbull barked beneath its slightly lopsided particle mask.

The damned thing needed a bath, Stone thought, and then felt himself an idiot, worrying about a dog's toilette when half the world was burning around them. He turned the switch of the big Harley, and its instant ignition system worked perfectly, roaring the engine to life. He looked over at the still functioning tank, the one remaining Bradley III, with all the latest armaments, including a missile system and radar/laser guidance tracking.

He was glad it was on his side. Stone knew what the war machine was capable of. General Patton had been planning to conquer America with a fleet of them, à la Rommel in the African desert. And the Fascist madman might well have succeeded—if he wasn't part of that swirling black cloud now. Stone gave the thumbs-up and saw Bull's face, dimly peering back from within the tank, give him the return signal. He hadn't trusted the big country boy back at boot camp, when Stone had infiltrated the general's main camp. But now that they had been through one mini-war, one near execution, and one hydrogen bomb blast together, Stone trusted Bull implicitly. And that went for the other three NAA recruits who were still left. If they'd been through all this already and still hadn't killed Stone with a shot to the back—or split with their weapons and all—then they sure as hell weren't going to do it now. For better or worse, Martin Stone was amassing his own little private army, though his combat power of one tank, one motorcycle, one dog, and a bunch of angry Indians would have to improve significantly if he was really going to make any headway as a military power.

Stone didn't even look back as he started the bike across the flat prairie, away from the cloud of doom that blotted out the dawn's feeble light. The sun tried to climb up into the black shroud that filled the northern skies of Colorado. But things didn't look too promising. The tank fell in behind Stone, following about twenty yards behind as Excaliber bedded down low on the back of the Harley's long leather seat, gripping his front and back legs around the thing like a starfish around an oyster. His right front leg had been wounded by Patton's troops. But with the splint that Stone had put on it, and the remarkable recuperative powers of the pitbull breed, the canine was already using it, putting pressure on it to hold itself in place atop the tearing cycle.

The Cheyenne looked hastily among themselves as the white men departed.

"Bah, we go north, past the cloud." Leaping Elk snorted contemptuously, waving his burned hand at the towering mushroom cloud to the north.

"No, we go with Stone," Meyra said softly but imperiously. She sat down in the slung-back seat of her three-wheeler, a heavy-duty cross-country vehicle with machine gun mounted on front, and started the engine. The rest of the small tribe was torn between Leaping Elk's mad show of bravery and scorn for the world of the white man and Meyra's simple but strong command. She was a descendant in the line of the Succession of the Chiefs. Only she was a *woman*. There had never been a woman chief among the Cheyennes. It made the braves feel peculiar, less than men, as they rushed to their all-terrains and started them up. But, taking off one after another, they fell in a long, ragged line behind her. At last there was just Leaping Elk and his own dummy, a shorter and fatter Indian who seemed to follow his every word and glance.

Leaping Elk continued to hold his badly burned hand up as he compared it against the mushroom cloud, seeking only he knew what sort of dark, aesthetic understanding. As the fleeting force of tanks and three-wheelers almost disappeared a mile off, its dust trail rising up slowly in the air, the Cheyenne, much to the relief of his lackey, mounted his bike and started off in pursuit.

Stone, in the lead, quickly found that he had to slow down from his forty miles per hour or the cloud of bomb dust that he sent up positively blinded anyone coming up behind him. He slowed to twenty, which helped a little, but it was still rough going. He hoped the others had their bandannas pulled tight and that the tank had been put on internal oxygen supply. Behind him, the pitbull nuzzled deeper into the space between the back of Stone's leather jacket and the leather of the seat—as if the air coming from there were cleaner than what was flowing all around them.

As the prairie came into view in the slight morning, Stone

saw to his disgust that the land had been decimated by the
blast. The sun was having a hard time getting much light
or warmth at all through the high cover of dark, radioactive fallout that was spreading out in a wider and wider
dome like an umbrella now, perhaps forty miles across.
But the little light that did filter through showed him just
what the results of a ten-megaton blast were on planet
earth. And it was terrible. Like beholding the rage of a
jealous god.

Every standing object had been torn down. Not that there
had been a hell of a lot of junk out there. But what little
there had been—cacti, scraggly trees—had been torn from
their roots and turned into smoking salad. They lay on their
sides in pieces of burned plant fiber, steaming, shrunken
roots reaching up toward the sky like a thousand skeletal
fingers in anguished vegetable prayer. The entire area was
covered with a layer of white powder, as if a snow had
fallen. But this stuff was crystallized sand, or maybe something else, Stone figured as he rode over it. He could feel the
warm clouds of heat rising up around him.

For the first few miles, most of the animal life he saw
were just piles of ash—hard to tell if it was even animal or
vegetable—or just mounds of ash and dirt congealed into
bumps in the earth. But when they had gotten thirty-five,
then forty miles away from ground zero, he could at least
make out what kind of creatures they had been. Elk with
their hides smoldering in dark, charred circles as if cigarettes
had been put out in them in a hundred places. Heads—just
skulls with horns still intact atop them, but blackened, almost shiny, as if coated with a high-gloss paint. A herd of
northern bison came into view as he peaked the top of a rise
and started down again. They were all grouped around one
another, as if they had been trying to seek protection from
the blast—pull in the wagons as it were—as they had
formed a loose sort of wedge with the strongest males in
front and the females behind. Then the calves huddled in the
safety of the thickest part of the defensive formation.

Not that it had done them a bit of good, of course. They
were all dead, half-burned corpses. Oddly, though parts of
them had been consumed into black leather, other parts were

nearly untouched. As Stone drove past them, Excaliber looked up from his cocoon and let out a plaintive howl. He recognized something in them. Some animal energy that had been consumed in the atomic fires. And in his own way he mouthed a mournful prayer from one creature to another, all of which were stuck on the most fucked-up planet in the universe.

Stone was struck by the haunting features the burning atomic winds had sculpted onto the dead bisom. There *was* an art of death: the way the heads on some were totally unscathed; their eyes still glassy and bright; other's heads nothing but blackened stumps spitting up boiling blood from time to time, while the bodies beneath them were virtually untouched, thick brown matted hair hanging down around the corpses. It had all depended on exactly what angle the bomb's rays and heat waves had reached them. It was like a panorama from the Museum of Natural History that Stone remembered visiting with his father, Major Clayton Stone, when he had been a child. The long, echoing marble rooms as big as a palace in a dream, and windows filled with scenes from all over the world—animals frozen forever in their dioramic habitat of plastic trees and paper moons.

"A museum of death," Stone muttered to himself as he looked at the mix of decay and wholeness, blood and fur. Some of the irradiated creatures appeared almost comical, with whole bodies and heads but nothing but bones for legs. Others like something from a nightmare, their faces melted into porridge as Little Bear's had been. Others even worse . . .

Stone spat down through his bandanna onto the prairie floating past him and pulled his eyes away from the death scene. He knew it was easy to get hypnotized by the dark beauty of destruction. But only madness lay that way.

To the south he could see mountains, but it was hard to tell how far away they were, since a haze caused by the dust the winds of the bomb had spread hung in the air like a curtain. Behind him—Stone turned around every ten or twenty minutes just to keep an eye on the course of the thing—the mushroom cloud was slowly spreading out, still in no great hurry. The light winds were pushing it to the south and east, as the top of the cloud still pushed its way into the very upper reaches of the stratosphere. When the damn thing came down, it could poison all of Colorado. Stone felt a deep bitterness start to rise up in him. The bastards just never got enough. The madmen, the Fascists, the destroyers of the world. They had to keep kicking at the planet till they blew her into little glowing pebbles and set her in orbit around the moon.

His glance was suddenly taken by a strange sight to the left of the course he was following. It looked as if hundreds of branches had been laid out in lines parallel to one another. And then, as he got closer, Stone saw that it was even weirder than that. The branches were snakes, and they were all dead. Cooked to a crisp, like fricasseed weiners. Their mouths were open wide, as if they had died gasping for air, and their bodies were all stretched out as far as they could go in a north-south direction. The outer edges of their skin had been turned a dark brown, like something that had been under the broiler for about half an hour.

Excalibar barked as if wanting to jump down, investigate, maybe have a snack or two. But Stone yelled around to the pitbull, "Sit down, you maniac. If you move one fucking inch—" Excaliber lowered himself back down on the seat but made a deep throaty sound, as if to say, "Then it better be chow time—and soon." Stone realized the snakes must have been driven from their holes by the heat and then tried to escape the rays by turning in the direction of the blast and hyperventilating. Of course, nothing had worked.

Stone glanced back when he was a few hundred yards farther on and could see dimly through the dust clouds that some of the Cheyenne were reaching down as they drove past and over the cooked snakes, grabbing a few for later dining. He winced involuntarily but didn't slow. These guys were *all* crazy, he decided. That was for damn sure.

It was when they had gotten beyond the direct bomb damage and fatalities that the injuries really got to Stone. For here, the wildlife had been wounded but not killed. They passed dozens, often hundreds, of limping, writhing, growling, crying-out animals. Armadillos, field rats, deer, bison, bears, raccoons, lizards, snakes—all screaming for merciful deliverance from a pain they neither understood nor could cure. A pain that already made their fur start to fall out, their teeth topple like rotting acorns, their guts turn to bloody stew inside their stomachs. They bared their teeth half-heartedly at the mini-fleet as the men drove past, and Stone had the urge to get down from his Harley and put some of them out of their misery. But there were too many. Too damn many by far. What was he going to do, perform merciful acts for the whole fucking world? Clean up after the death wish of mankind had been released each time? Forget it, pal. Not today.

Still, he was hardly able to look at the suffering creatures and had to hold his eyes like steel marbles straight ahead on the course he was following—due south. His mouth tightened as he hardened himself to a cruel world, and to the cruelty that men must allow themselves to endure just to survive.

But when they reached the first of the low hills that quickly led to a full-fledged range a few miles off, Stone saw suddenly that it was mankind he was going to have to worry about a lot more than the animals. Namely his own ass. He had just gone into a low valley about a hundred feet wide with small grassy hills rising on each side when he saw them: men coming down from the slopes ahead on horses, mules, and all sorts of ragged-looking mounts. The horses looked better than their riders. A filthier bunch of detoothed, scarred, and pockmarked faces sitting atop fat, greasy bodies Stone could hardly recall having seen.

He came to a stop as the rest of the column fell in behind him, until his Harley, the tank, and the eight three-wheelers of the Cheyenne formed a rough wedge so they all had firing clearance at the primitive cavalry.

"Well, what have we here?" The leader apparent of the raiding party laughed from atop his barrel-chested steed. The horse looked like it could pull a tractor; so did its master. "A pretty sorry-looking bunch, if I do say so myself." The man laughed, and his entire frame of four hundred and fifty plus pounds shook from side to side, as his gnarled face—which looked like it had been through a hundred fights, a dozen bitings, and at least a few acid burnings—scrunched up in amusement, an expression Martin Stone didn't like at all. He looked back and forth to both sides of the valley, where the bandits sat atop their various mounts. There were at least forty to the right, and two dozen on the left side of the valley floor, down which Stone and his crew had been heading.

"Have you taken a good look at yourself recently?" Stone asked, pulling his hand back on the right handlebar so it rested near the firing trigger of the .50-caliber machine gun mounted on the front of his Harley.

"No, I haven't taken a look at myself," the jowled tub of boil-ridden lard yelled back. "There isn't too many mirrors around these parts on account of they've all been broken. People use 'em for knives. But I knows I ugly, anyway." The man laughed, and his friends on each side howled along with him. "Shoot, everybody in these parts knows I is the ugliest man in Colorado."

"He so ugly, his mama puked all over him the second he popped out of her belly!" One of the nearby riders laughed through toothless lips. The leader of the group, apparently a devotee of humor only when it was originated by him, leaned to the side of his steed so that it almost toppled over and slammed out a bear-sized fist, sweeping the speaker right off his mule and onto the dirt. The man looked up, mortified, but didn't dare say a word.

"Say what you want about me, boys—but no one talks about my mama. Bless her soul." He crossed himself, then, smilingly sweetly, he turned back to Stone.

"Before I was so rudely interrupted," the man went on, sweeping his arm toward Stone as if he were bowing, as if he had manners or etiquette, which was just about the most absurd thing imaginable, since the fat pig of a Warlord was covered with grease and matted food from head to foot. Flies buzzed constantly around his long beard, trying to suck out food lodged in there; snot caked his sleeves where he had been wiping it for years. "I was about to introduce myself. "I am Colonel William Beausmont, King of Cheshard. Welcome to my country."

Stone looked around him as if surveying the place. Then back at the "king" atop his overburdened packhorse, red sores all around the animal's sides and ribs from the huge weight above it and the constant spurring of the animal with the obese man's boots. "Place could use a little landscaping," Stone muttered. "Looks like shit, if you want to know the truth."

"Ah, a man who speaks the truth," the tub of lies burped back, as he almost spat up some of the food he had eaten that morning. "So refreshing when all those around me"—he looked around at his motley crew as if it were *they* who were foul and *he* covered with rose petals —"are bastards, liars, and double-dealing scum of the highest—or should I say, lowest order? Thus I will speak the truth to you, little man," Beausmont went on, scratching at his beard, which hung down over his chest as if there were something trapped in there. Stone wouldn't have been surprised to see something leap out and go slithering off. "I'll let you live—we're not murderers around here—but you've got to pay. You know what I mean—good old-fashioned American capitalism. I have a product. You buy it. Everyone is happy."

"And just what product are you selling?" Stone asked with a cynical grunt as he edged his fingers just a trace closer to the trigger of his hidden machine gun. Excaliber growled ominously behind him, and Stone hissed him silent with a sharp but low sound out of the corner of his mouth. The dog set down again, but Stone could feel him quivering the way he always did before an attack. *Don't move, dog,* Stone commanded it mentally, *or I'll kill you.* Whether it heard him or not, it quieted down slightly.

"Selling these." The king of lard laughed good-naturedly, taking out some sort of medallion from inside his jacket. He held it up to Stone to show him it wasn't a bomb or anything, and then threw it across the fifteen or so yards separating them. Stone caught it in the air and looked down at it. The object was preposterous. The end of a soda can that had been flattened, a crude chain put through its pop top so it could be worn around the neck.

"It's safe passage through these parts," the filthy leader of the mountain bandits went on, sweeping his eyes over Stone's force as if trying to visually pry out the goodies. The muzzle of the Bradley III tank and the cold stares of a half dozen Indians took some of the smile off his face. But still he went on loudly, now staring with little ice picks toward Stone, trying to intimidate him. "You wear one of these, you get through. You don't, you're dead. It's that simple. We got men throughout these hills—ain't no one gets through without paying. Our range extends for two hundred miles to the south. After that, you're in somebody else's territory. That's their problem—and yours. But it ain't mine."

"This is America, pal," Stone said almost quietly but with a force that they all heard. "There are no separate countries or kingdoms. No safe passages. That's the thing about this country—you can go where you want."

"Used to be friend, used to be," the bandit leader went on, scratching his balls as he spoke. "But them's the old days, these is the new days—and *we* rule here. So give me some guns and bullets or we cut your balls to chop suey." He looked around him, sweeping his hand across his rows of horse-mounted fighters who had belts of slugs draped around their shoulders like mail armor, pistols, and sawed-off mini-autos dangling from saddles everywhere. The ugly bastards looked like they were ready for war. But so was Martin Stone.

"Don't you see this tank?" Stone asked, standing up now on the side kicks of his bike, so they could all clearly see and hear him. If fatso was going to be dramatic up there on his horse, Stone knew he had to create a similar sort of power scene from his end. "Don't you assholes know what a tank can do?"

"Seen lots of ve-hi-cles 'round these parts," the mountain king went on, slapping up at the flies that buzzed around his lips. "Seen tanks, too—but not a one of them could fire, or assholes in 'em who knew how to make 'em do it."

"Well, that's not the situation here," Stone said as coldly as glacial ice. "That tank can fire. And so can I—and these Cheyenne here. And we can take out your whole damn crew. Believe me. I'm not bullshitting you. So let's put it this way," Stone went on, catching Bull's attention in the tank some ten feet behind out of the corner of his eye, signaling him to get ready. "*You* get out of our way right now and we'll just say the whole thing was a mistake. Otherwise . . ."

"Otherwise? Otherwise?" The bandit king seemed stunned by the implied threat. He wasn't used to being challenged. Not for a long, long time. He raised his hands in the air as if to implore the gracious heavens above not to send him such fools to deal with. Then his hands came down fast, and a pump shotgun appeared from out beneath his mismatched coon-and-bearskin coat. Flame was blasting out of it before even Stone could move.

Then all hell broke loose. Stone dropped back down to the seat of the Harley, flat on his stomach, and pulled the trigger of the .50-caliber on the front frame. The weapon exploded into a hail of slugs just as the shotgun blast reached the motorcycle. The wall of pellets slammed into the dirt near his right leg, a few of them ricocheting up from the rocks and through Stone's fatigues, making him grunt for a second in pain. There was a roar just behind his right ear as the Bradley's huge cannon erupted out a 120-mm shell. A funnel of air and smoke *whooshed* out behind the sudden pressure release of the two-foot-long shell, and Stone smelled the wave of cordite odor sweep over him.

The tank shell hardly had time to get going before it slammed into the king's fur-covered chest. At the range of twenty-five feet, the shell was traveling at such high speed that it tore through his chest and into his backbone before the detonator encountered just enough resistance to detonate. The mountain murderer and his horse were blown in a hundred different directions, sending scores of their fellow bandits and mounts flying down like bloody bowling pins. Screams and whinnies of terror filled the air even above the cracks of pistols and automatic weapons.

Stone raised his head just enough to see the ranks of horsemen trying to get a bead on them. He swept the 50-caliber back and forth across the bandits—and they fell like moths in a backyard light clumsily to the earth. Here and there the horses took shots, too, and reared back, kicking around in the dirt. Others threw their riders and tore off up the valley slope to escape. Again the Bradley roared, and Stone found it so deafening that he couldn't hear a thing. Everything was suddenly occurring in absolute silence, so it almost looked beautiful, a ballet of fire and death—the flames and puffs of smoke coming from all directions, the shells from the tank going off about thirty yards to the left, dead center of a large formation of the attackers.

The group disappeared for a moment in an eruption of flame and dirt, and as it quickly cleared, men and horses were flying off as if in a race with death, a race most of them had just lost. They tumbled through the air, broken, with missing arms, flanks, heads, from the sheer force of the blast. Blood sprewed out from the newly created holes in jets of purest red.

And just like that, it was over. Half their force dead in ten seconds, the rest of the stunned bandits looked around in terror at each other, turned, and ran. They were animals now—without their leader, who lay in flakes somewhere. Beyond pride, beyond anything, they just wanted to survive.

Stone held his arms up as the remaining horses and their riders scrambled up and over the valley slopes, telling his men not to fire. The Bradley ceased its thunderous volleys, and after a few more pops, so did the Cheyenne behind him. Ammunition was too precious a commodity to waste in the murderous landscape that was America. Within seconds all the bandits were gone, and only the dead or pieces of them were left, strewn around the ground as if a picnic of vampires and werewolves had just finished using the area.

"I warned them," Stone muttered to the afternoon wind as it brought the scent of horseflesh to his already burning nostrils. "Don't say I didn't warn them." He looked up at the afternoon sky, which was already growing dark, as if pleading with it. The atmosphere was filling with high clouds that seemed to glow in the twilight, the dimmest of electric auras around their mountainous shapes.

Stone started the Harley forward and past the charnal grounds as the rest of the men followed on their vehicles. Not one of them talked. The annihilation was too complete, too fast to feel particularly heroic about. Only Leaping Elk, taking up the rear, laughed and hummed to himself as he slowed to look at the pieces of bodies, fingers, and eyeballs floating around in the blood-soaked prairie sands. He seemed to get a big kick out of it all, chuckling over each little mutilation, each severed part. At last, tiring of it, he floored his cross-country and shot out over the puddles of blood, spitting them up in a red mist behind him as he moved into the low hills after the others.

It took only minutes after the battle, after Stone and his men had departed, for the predators to emerge from their wretched holes. Hundreds of them at first, then thousands, came up out of countless little tunnels in the earth, brown, wriggling bodies that inundated the death grounds with blankets of hunger.

Cockroaches. Nature's most perfect creature. The oldest living thing on earth that has remained unchanged. The roach had seen the dinosaurs come and go. Big deal. Now nuclear weapons. But these roaches seemed to have thrived on a little atomic energy. Cockroaches are two thousand times as resistant to radiation as are humans. Thus this bunch, exposed to enough rads to kill any mammal, had only built up an appetite, like a sunburn can do to you after a long day at the beach. They came out with voracious little feelers, hardly believing their luck at stumbling upon the ocean of blood, the smorgasbord of human flesh. And so, being nature's most perfect creature, they dug in and filled their stomachs fast. As they could dimly remember in their genetic memories to a time when great, thundering lizards had once stampeded through the land, even the biggest dinner could disappear faster than you could grab a fork. The oldest truth of life on earth: Eat your food fast, before it runs away.

Chapter Three _____

S tone led them on into the darkening night. The full moon was but a dim cottonball in the far sky, and he had to switch on his headlights as the rest did the same behind him, sending out swaths of light that cut dusty tunnels through the filthy air. Even through the high-clad clouds Stone could see the aurora borealis undulating out in rippling sheets of magnetic color. The bomb blast had obviously shaken it all up, as the colors were far brighter than he had ever seen them—and the curtains extended as if into the heavens themselves. Excaliber growled behind him on the seat and seemed nervous, sensing somehow the momentary damage to the earth's magnetic field.

At last Stone made the decision to stop. They'd been going for days now, on the run, hiding from a nuke blast, then on the run again. It was too much for even the toughest of men to take forever. He came to a slow stop on a ridge that had a clear view from all sides. They could bivouac here and, with a guard, get a good night's sleep. They had all seen what their combined firepower could do. It made for an easier night's rest, if nothing else.

The force pulled into a defensive circle on the thirty-yard-wide plateau about twenty feet up from the surrounding land, the guns of every vehicle aimed outward and down, so that if there was an attack, they would be ready. The Bradley was turned on a dime in the center of the rise, its big 120-mm cannon facing out into the threatening night.

"You're getting pretty fucking good with that thing," Stone yelled up as Bull's big head popped out of the center of the turret.

"Jesus Christ!" Bull laughed, climbing up to the top of the Bradley III. "Being cooped up inside a tank for twenty hours is like learning to live inside a metal toilet bowl. I mean"—he nodded good-humoredly back at the others who followed up behind the tank captain as he jumped down to the ground—"these guys stink."

Stone smiled. "Stink is the perfume of battle, pal. Be glad you're still able to sweat. It means you're alive. The dead can't smell themselves rot. Only the living have that pleasure."

"Keep stinking, keep stinking." Bull laughed as he lifted his arm and poked his nose under it, taking a deep whiff. Even some of the usually stone-faced Cheyenne laughed at that. The men seemed to get along pretty well, Stone had come to see, except for that son of a bitch, Leaping Elk. The rest of the band seemed perfectly willing to let the past lie where it may and start anew on an equal footing with the white man. But the half-crazed brave couldn't let it lie.

It started up again as they ate, seated around a low, crackling fire just off to one side of the tank. Stone had warned them about eating the snakes, promising them better food than that, anyway. He had promptly gone off and bagged a small elk in the woods with his .44 Redhawk, taking it out with one fast shot to the head. The skull of the mountain elk was almost gone, but the body, the meat, was untouched. Back at the bivouac, Stone let the Indians expertly slice the thing up and throw it in thin strips over a grill on the fire. Within minutes they were chewing down a delicious if primitive dinner, eating the strips in their hands, washed down with mouthfuls of water from their canteens or water gourds. Excaliber ate his three strips in a second flat and looked up, mouth panting wildly for more. He was on thirds before all the men had even finished their first helpings. But there was plenty to go around. No one needed to feel greedy.

Just when Stone's battered brain and churning stomach were starting to settle down, Leaping Elk had to inject some psychosis into the proceedings. He took a piece of the meat, chewed it for a few seconds, and then, standing up, spat it into the fire near Stone's feet, where the bloody minute steak sputtered softly in the flames.

"How Cheyenne can eat meat killed by a white man, this I cannot understand," the tall, lanky Indian said contemptuously, staring hard at the others. They watched him but didn't stop chewing. If it took a tongue-lashing to keep eating, so be it. Leaping Elk whipped his other hand out of the shadows and held up one of the gamma-rayed, bug-eyed snakes they had passed earlier.

"Eat this. The desert provides for us. *This* will give us strength."

"The desert didn't provide that," Stone said softly between chews, praying that this wasn't going to escalate into a scene and he would have to stop eating, get up, and get into a fight with a fucking insane Indian. "An atomic bomb did. And everything touched by that bomb is deadly. Is poison. You eat that and you're a dead man."

"Dead?" The Cheyenne laughed as he turned dramatically in front of the eating men. "Why am I not dead from this, then?" He waved his atomically burned hand, which had swelled up to double its normal size, the fingers like red cigars, the palm huge and distended like a catcher's mitt, all purple and spotted. Even the hungriest of Cheyenne had to look away as he ate. "See, I absorb its poisons. That is the Indian way. You defeat all that challenges you. You kill it—and absorb it. Its energy becomes you. You become it." He waved his burned hand high above his head, staring at it as if looking into the face of God, and did a strange little dance. Then he lifted the stiff polelike snake to his lips and took a huge bite, chomping down hard on the cooked flesh. They all heard the crack as his teeth snapped through the cartilage. Leaping Elk gulped hard as the head and neck of the snake slowly disappeared into his grinding mouth.

After four bites he reached down into the darkness and took up a handful of stiff snakes, throwing the spears of frozen, high-rad snake chow out over to them.

"Eat it! You hear me! I command you to eat of the

snake!" The Cheyenne was in a frenzy of some kind now, his face all red, his eye twice as big as normal, his mouth dripping at both corners, a white, bubbling foam that seemed to come from deep within.

"Stop it," a voice suddenly said, cutting through the night, and for a second there was shocked silence, only the snap of the fire piercing the air as they all turned to Meyra, who had stood up in sudden anger at Leaping Elk's attempts to bully them all with his madness. "You hear me," she said, staring hard at him across the ten feet or so that separated the two. They were the only ones standing, the rest of the Cheyenne and Stone's men still chewing away as they watched the little drama unfold. Excaliber, in seventh heaven, quickly went after Meyra's food when he saw it unguarded at her feet. He disappeared with five whole strips into the shadows, from which slurping sounds of something trying to eat far more than it possibly could emerged for several seconds.

The two Indians locked eyes in silence, and they could all feel the pure energy of two wills in combat streaking between the pair. Stone let his hand drop to his side so it was near his Ruger—just in case. He knew it wouldn't be good politics to drop the Cheyenne in his tracks. But if the loony attacked Meyra, Stone wouldn't think twice, let the chips fall where they may.

"You don't run things around here," Leaping Elk said, his voice as cold as a hit man's, his eyes suddenly focused and very calculating.

"Nor you," Meyra snapped back. "If my brother was alive, you would have not dared act so stupid."

"It is not stupid," the Cheyenne said, suddenly enraged, as he raised himself to his full six-feet-four. "The eating of the snakes is the Old Way. We must stick with the Old Ways —the new ones will kill us. We will no longer be Indians but white man. We will lose the magic, the medicine. The snakes, the snakes . . ." Now he seemed to go completely mad as his face twitched and blood oozed out of the radiated hand in a sudden gush. He threw snakes at her, at all of them, threw the stiff bodies like little spears, reaching down again and again.

"Eat them, do you hear me?" And when he was done and could find no more of the fried snake jerky, he looked at her with an even stranger grin than before and, suddenly lowering his pants, snarled out, "And you can eat this. You hear me, bitch woman? You can have this." He waved his organ in his radioactive hand, hefting it like some kind of metaphysical weapon of the sexes.

Meyra's face grew contorted, so filled with rage did she become. She rushed the few feet separating them with the speed of a leopard, shouting all the way.

"Goddamn right I will, pig. Goddamn right." He raised his hands to grab her as she rushed up to him, but the twisted smile on his half-lipped face suddenly turned to a scream as her knee came up under him. She slammed the bony kneecap up into the Cheyenne's testicles with the force of a cannonball, and the large Indian took off right up into the air as if he'd been launched from a silo. He must have risen a good two feet straight off the ground before he fell back to earth, landing on his side where he writhed and screamed in exquisite agony.

"Don't talk to me about the Old Ways, you pig." Meyra sneered down at him, curling her lips back in utter disgust. "You dirty the name of Indian. No real Cheyenne would ever have done something like that. Crawl off, vermin, away from me." Leaping Elk's lackey helped drag him off into the shadows, as the Indian couldn't even raise himself up off the ground. She had hurt him bad. And Stone knew a man like that was the most dangerous of all.

She looked back at the other Cheyenne. "I know I'm a woman. And I know you're all tough macho men who couldn't stand to break a thousand years of tradition and let a woman run things. But that's not what I want. My brother's dead, but I'm not going to follow this maniac. And if any of you do, you're as insane as him. He sullies the name Cheyenne." The others nodded and grunted in agreement as they sucked at their teeth and reached for a final piece or two of the meat. They did respect him. Leaping Elk definitely had the crazy wisdom in his veins. But he was too crude. Too much animal in him. None of them wished to die, and they could see, could feel, that that was where he was heading—and fast.

"Let's try to do things in a more democratic way. You know, we'll decide things together, vote on them. Perhaps the old ways are gone forever. Perhaps they're no good any longer." They looked at her and one another noncommittally. The idea was too radical, too new.

"I'm going to leave for a few hours," Stone said when they were all satiated and lying around the fire with dumb smiles on their faces. The NAA recruits and the Indians shared a jug of gin one of the men pulled out, and seemed to be getting along all right. Stone had purposely wanted to wait until they were all too full and lazy to move. There would be no more trouble tonight, though he knew there wasn't a hell of a lot holding the whole fighting force together.

"I'm going to get some medicine for us," Stone went on as all eyes focused sleepily on his shape, silhouetted by the orange heat waves of the cooking fire. "Anti-rad pills. My father stashed them not that far from here. I'll be back before dawn. We need them. The radiation is already running through our veins, in our lungs. There are ways to neutralize it—if we move fast, real fast. 'Cause though I'm sure all of you are skeptical as hell, we're in a race against time already. Death is waiting up in those skies, in those clouds, as surely as it's already streaming through our bodies at this very moment."

Chapter Four _____

The hard hand of the night slapped against Stone's face as the north wind blew across the lower mountains of the Rockies. But he didn't push the painful sensations away—in fact, he welcomed anything to get his mind off all the problems confronting him—the radiation, the feuding Cheyenne, April . . . Every minute he was alive, things seemed to get more complicated.

"Fuck!" he spat out into the wind. It felt good to scream it. "Fuck, fuck, fuck." He didn't even know exactly who he was angry at—maybe at the whole goddamn world. But Excaliber apparently shared similar feelings. For he joined in howling out his own canine profanities along with his master, gripping the seat hard with all four limbs as he bayed up into the night, into the cold air above.

The sky was getting stranger all the time, Stone noticed as he bounced around the seat of the droning Harley as it shot up and down mountain roads at a good clip. The colors of the aurora were truly bizarre tonight—reds and violets and greens, like some sort of dark rainbow. The phantasmagoric pulsations ran back and forth from the earth to the uppermost reaches of the atmosphere in rippling patterns of energy. The whole sky looked like it was on fire. The earth was unsettled and vomiting out her magnetic rage at being nuked.

But it was the rows of burning yellow eyes along both sides of the mountain road that caught Stone's attention. For he knew they had teeth attached to them. Timber wolves, a pack of them. By the number of blazing eyes he knew there were a lot. Must have been driven off by the blast and congregated together in one huge hunting unit. Within seconds the glowing orbs were on all sides of him, and Stone could hear the growls coming from the shadows, from behind the trees. Growls that quickly turned to barks as the wolf pack argued among itself about whether or not to attack. Excaliber stood up, his fur bristling, his jaws pulled back to crocodilian proportions. The pitbull let out with a heart-stopping growl and then another, baring his fangs in a smile of, "If you're gonna boogie, come on, mother, do it." He and his breed, Stone had learned, much to his dismay, never shrank from a good fight. Especially against fifty or more wolves. Why, the night was just beginning.

But the pitbull's challenge unsettled the wolves just long enough for Stone to pull back on the throttle so the Harley accelerated from thirty to seventy in three seconds. The front wheel lifted off as he tore down the road, his headlight slicing back and forth through the darkness ahead like a sword. The wolves gathered themselves and tried to head the bike off, the ones farthest ahead darting in at a sharp angle to try to stop it.

"Down," Stone screamed out to the bullterrier, which he could feel was sort of half hanging on to the back of the bike, getting ready to jump off and into the thick of it. "Get your fucking ass down or I leave you here," Stone screamed in his most commanding tones. He didn't have time to play around. The dog whined and sat back down with a thump of anger. It kept its head on the seat but its jaws open, in case one of them got close enough to take a nip out of.

Stone saw the shapes hurtle from both sides simultaneously—big ones, by the light of the beam. Their fur bristled silver in the reflection, and they grew closer until Stone could feel their musky breath upon him, their jaws reaching out. But leaning far forward on the bike, at that speed, Stone was more like a projectile than a person. The front bars and low windbreak of the Harley slammed into the two 175-pounders like they were made out of paper. The pair of timber wolves went flying backward in the direction from

which they had come, both of them out cold, spinning
around in the air, blood whipping from their mouths and
ears. One more wolf tried a final, futile leap, thinking he
could be the hero of the hunt. It was his last mistake. The
screaming 1200-cc was going seventy-five by the time it had
gone fifty yards. The wolf came head on toward the bike as
if playing a game of Chicken.

Vehicle hit predator, and one went flying. The wolf exploded off to the side, one whole side of its neck severed
open so it leaked out thick red blood like a broken pipe in a
basement. Stone almost lost control of the bike as it bounced
to the right from the impact, digging in at a steep angle. But
throwing one foot down as they were about to go over at
high speed, he was able to bounce the bike right back off the
prairie floor like a stone bouncing off a pond. The Harley
shot a straight course ahead, but there were no more takers.
Stone could feel the yellow eyes burning into his back without looking around.

He was glad to see he had correctly gauged the distance
to his father, Major Clayton's, hidden mountain bunker in
the northern hills of Estes National Park. He had figured two
and a half to three hours. But with his ass being goosed by
the wolf attack, he had trimmed it down to just over two.
Stone hit the country road, an ancient one-laner that was
already cracking into a thousand threads of concrete from
the harsh winters and broiling summers and the lack of the
slightest repairs. Five miles on this and then he turned off
into what to the passerby could only have seemed like a
dense bunch of bushes and brambles. But by pushing aside
the barbed branches he was able to get through the ten feet
or so of mini-jungle, sealing it behind him. He moved off at
about twenty miles per hour down the almost invisible path
through a series of hills covered with low brush and fir trees.

At last Stone reached the sheer side of a mountain wall
and pulled the bike to a stop. He dismounted, the auto kickstand popping out in a flash so the bike stayed upright on its
own. Excaliber opened one eye and, seeing nothing particularly exciting going on, at least at that moment, closed it
again to get another few seconds of nod on its schedule.
When Stone reached the boulder in the ground that hid the

transmitter allowing entrance to the bunker, he knew instantly that someone had been there. He had been attacked just days before, by a Mafia hit squad of assassins. But he had been positive they had followed him directly in and that no one else knew about the place. Yet the huge football-shaped boulder had definitely been rolled back at a slightly different angle than he had left it.

He budged the heavy rock aside, looking down cautiously into the three-foot hole below, to make sure there wasn't a bomb or such planted there. He had learned that complete and total paranoia was the best policy out here in the lawless lands. But the transmitter, wrapped in a plastic bag, was the only object in the dirt hole, and Stone carefully lifted it and aimed it at the solid rock face. He pressed a switch, and the very sides of the mountain wall seemed to slide apart as two three-foot-thick doors of solid granite slid apart, creating a wide entrance. Stone mounted the bike and drove it in, the walls closing behind him automatically, as they were programmed to do unless receiving a counter-instruction within ten seconds. He parked the bike alongside the two cars and a van parked in the outer garage of the bunker.

"Home" again. It still made him feel weird every time he came in the damn place. "Come on, dog!" Stone put his fingers in his lips and let loose with a sharp blast that made the pitbull's ears instantly perk up like flags rising on a flagpole, as its eyes opened as wide as omelets. It looked at Stone as if to say, "That wasn't fair," and then rose and jumped down off the bike. Realizing where it was, the animal suddenly sped up and rushed ahead of Stone. It knew the way by heart, and the moment he opened the front door that led into the main house, the animal had disappeared in a blur and headed down the hall, through the living room and into the kitchen. The goddamn mutt was nothing more than a trained Pavlovian rat, Stone thought with disgust—behaviorized into making all the right turns to get to its beloved chow.

As he walked through the living room Stone's gaze swept around the entire space, still clean and spotless, with its large loftlike area, its plants, plush wall-to-wall carpeting, thick caressing couches. In his mind he kept seeing them all sitting there, his mother knitting, his father reading military tales or Kipling stories, his sister writing her poetry on her computer or doodling with her MacPaint. Happy little family scene, Stone thought as he blinked his eyes and rubbed them hard.

Ghosts. Ghosts of the past. Would he ever be rid of them? They seemed to cling to him like a spiderweb, wet and sticky and suffocating. They had all lived together for five years inside the ultramodern hole in the side of a mountain, twenty thousand square feet plus of every imaginable convenience, fully stocked kitchen, armaments room, private bedrooms, firing range . . . The Major had been prepared, that was for damn sure, Stone thought as a little grin passed over his face. Now that the son of a bitch was dead, Martin found himself actually caring about his old man a lot more than he had done when the Major had been alive. Then they had done nothing but argue. For years. Even as they lived together in the bunker there had been an electric tension between them as Major Clayton R. Stone, Ret., had tried to teach his son *his* ways—and Martin had resisted. Now that the old man was dead, Stone could allow himself softer memories of the past. It all became hazy, events a little funnier, his father a little less of a person and more of a myth, a dream that had happened in another life, a dream Stone held in his head like a haunting hologram.

Stone blinked again, and the ghosts disappeared, vanishing from the couches, the rug. He walked through the wide living space and then down a long hallway to his father's main computer room. The instant he touched the door, he knew something was up.

It was ajar. Yet when he had left it just days before, he had closed it—and it required a punched-in combination on a computer keypad to the right of the doorway to gain entrance. Stone pulled out his .44 Magnum and held it loosely at solar plexus level, eyeing every corner of the beeping, pulsing room. His father had been a computer buff—even a genius, perhaps—and had filled this, his private chamber, with nearly a million dollars worth of computers, processing gear, and communications devices. God knew what all. The preprogrammed setup was still carrying out all sorts of func-

tions on its own, powered by computer-run electric genera-
tors and a combination of solar and gasoline power, for
which his father had once told him the place could fuel itself
for ten years without a single drop being added. Then it
would die—as dead as the mountain rock itself.

But for the moment the room appeared to be functioning
perfectly. Everywhere were green and amber blinking lights,
numbers buzzing across screens, sine waves and graphs,
clicking sounds as radio transmissions were automatically
tape-recorded. Stone could see no one. Somehow he knew
that if someone was hiding here, he would sense them. Yet
he felt nothing. He went to the main computer console, sat
down, laid the big .44 up on the Formica table, and entered
the "on" code. The screen blinked to life, and the moment it
did, a red light blinked on and off and the words EMER-
GENCY COMMUNICATION, EMERGENCY COMMUNICATION gal-
loped across it in flickering letters.

Stone stared up in amazement as lines of glowing green
print begin advancing down the face of the wide glass monitor in front of him:

> MARTIN, THIS IS APRIL. I CAN ONLY HOPE THAT
> IT'S YOU WHO IS READING THIS. BUT YOU WOULD BE
> THE ONLY ONE WHO COULD ACCESS THE CRAY II. I'M
> WITH DR. KENNEDY. BUT WE'RE BOTH IN GREAT
> DANGER. ALL OF US ARE. YOU TOO. THEY'RE AFTER
> US, MARTIN. A HIT TEAM, TRACKING US DOWN LIKE
> DOGS FROM THE MOMENT WE ESCAPED FROM THE
> DWARF'S RESORT. THE DOC WAS WOUNDED, BUT I
> THINK HE'LL LIVE. BUT WE CAN'T STAY HERE.
> THEY'RE TOO NEAR. WE'RE GOING TO RESUPPLY
> OURSELVES AND LEAVE. LEAVE IN THE MIDDLE OF
> THE NIGHT THROUGH THE EMERGENCY DOOR. MAR-
> TIN—WE'RE GOING TO GO TO THE PLACE WHERE YOU
> AND I VACATIONED WHEN WE WERE KIDS. YOU
> KNOW WHERE I MEAN—WHERE GRANDMOTHER
> LIVED OUT HER LAST YEARS. IT'S ISOLATED ENOUGH
> THAT NO ONE COULD FIND US. AND WE'LL WAIT FOR
> YOU. I PRAY THAT YOU'RE STILL ALIVE. IF YOU'RE
> NOT, I'M SURE THAT IT WON'T BE LONG UNTIL I JOIN

YOU IN WHATEVER THERE IS AFTER ALL
THIS—'CAUSE IT'S PRETTY FUCKING HORRIBLE
WHERE I'M STANDING. LOVE APRIL.

Yeah, that was sis, all right, Stone thought with a sardonic
twitch. Always the card, always the optimist. Always a way
with words to make you look on the bright side of things.
Not that it wasn't all true. So she had gone to their other
summer home in Stoneham in Pawnee National Park. If the
bunker was in remote territory, that place was ready for a
cover of *National Geographic*. It was high up on the side of
a mountain, right up in the goddamn clouds. It was only
twenty miles to the southeast but was inaccessible to anyone
without a pickax and a llama. If she made it, she'd be safe
—for the moment.

Stone keyed out the message and then asked for and got
access to general information—the main directory of his father's extensive computer-information system. When his father had set the system up, knowing his son might someday
need it, even have his life be dependent on the data, the
Major had tried to make it as simple and user-friendly as
possible. So all Stone had to do was pick a subject, then
zero in on more and more precise information.

"AREA OF INFORMATION?" the computer printed out on
the monitor in front of him.

"RADIATION," Stone typed in. The computer box on the
table was hooked up with parallel port cables to the mainframe, a Cray II Jr., the only computer that the Cray company had ever allowed to be sold to a private individual, his
father. But then, being a war hero, and the president and
main stockholder of one of the most powerful and influential
munitions manufacturing plants in the country, Major Clayton R. Stone, ex-Ranger, circa Special Forces, circa
LURPS, Vietnam, was not often a man who didn't get his
way.

"RADIATION," the computer terminal scrolled in a flash in
front of Stone. A list of subheadings about the subject
flashed on and off.

"MEDICAL TREATMENTS FOR:" Stone keyed in, and sat
back as the mainframe seemed to gulp down the information

with a little electronic bump on the far side of the large computer room.

"RADIATION POISONING." The green words began jumping across the screen almost as fast as Stone could read them. "EXPOSURE TO VARIOUS FORMS OF RADIATION FROM WASTE PRODUCT TO REACTOR MATERIALS TO BOMB DETONATION. TYPICALLY GAMMA RAYS, BETA PARTICLES, HEAT WAVES, SUFFICIENT TO CAUSE SIGNIFICANT TO TOTAL CELLULAR DISRUPTION AND/OR ANNIHILATION.

"HYDROGEN BOMB BLAST," the screen scrolled on. A chart appeared on the terminal of an H-bomb going off, and the computer asked Stone for its size.

"TEN MEGATONS," he keyed in. "DETONATION DISTANCE 25 MILES."

Within a second the screen was digitizing back. "CENTRAL LOCATION OF BLAST HERE." A flashing dot appeared on the monitor, and then concentric circles going outward from the explosion at ten-mile intervals. "DEAD ZONE," the inner ring read, as did the second one. "AT 30 AND 40 MILES," the monitor scrolled. "SEVERE POISONING FROM GAMMA RAYS. AT 50—SURVIVAL POSSIBLE. MAXIMUM TREATMENT NEEDED."

"SYMPTOMS: NAUSEA, BLEEDING FROM ALL ORIFICES, HAIR LOSS, TEETH LOSS, FINGERNAIL LOSS. PEELING OFF OF SKIN AND LIPS IS NOT UNCOMMON WITH RADIATION BURNS OF SEVERE MAGNITUDE. LEUKEMIA, CANCER OF ALL FORMS, BEGIN SHOWING UP WITHIN 6 TO 12 MONTHS.

"RADIATION MADNESS: OFTEN A KIND OF MADNESS CAN SET IN ON THOSE HEAVILY IRRADIATED BUT NOT KILLED OUTRIGHT. SYMPTOMS ARE SIMILAR TO RABIES, WITH FOAMING AT THE MOUTH AND VIOLENT, EVEN PSYCHOTIC, ACTIONS.

TREATMENTS: RECENT DISCOVERIES SHOW THAT POTASSIUM IODIDE, SEA KELP, AND CERTAIN MIXTURES OF VITAL MINERALS AND TRACE ELEMENTS CAN ACT AS POWERFUL CLEANSING AGENTS TO THE ENTIRE BODY. AS LONG AS THE SYSTEM IS FED THESE SUBSTANCES IT NEEDS, IT WILL NOT HAVE TO TAKE THEM FROM THE FOOD SOURCE OR THE AIR, BOTH OF WHICH WILL BE RADIOACTIVE.

"SUGGESTED PRESCRIPTIONS:

POTASSIUM IODIDE—20 MG PER DAY.

KELP TABLETS—100 MG PER DAY.

MIXED TRACE ELEMENTS AND VITAMINS—200 MG PER DAY."

The computer sped on and on, giving Stone more information on how to deal with radiation poisoning than he could deal with. From not eating any animals that grazed or fed on other animals for at least six months to not touching any but spring water for at least two months. He tried to note what he could but at last grew impatient, knowing he had to get the hell out of there. He knew what he had come to find out. He knew they had all been heavily saturated with radiation and were right now living in the spit-up of the big bomb. Unless they could clean out their systems internally, they were dead men. Whatever the Indians believed about the power of the Cheyenne spirits, it was the white man's poison that would kill them all.

Chapter Five _____

S tone swore he felt funny as he walked out of the computer room, this time shutting the steel door securely
behind him. He didn't know if it was reading about all
the stuff or what, but he swore he had all the symptoms—
every damn one of them. The strangest thing was his skin,
which felt all sunburned. Even his guts felt like they'd been
microwaved, everything all hot and threatening to spasm at
any moment. Stone moved fast to the medical supplies room
and quickly found the pills the computer had referred to. He
opened one of each of the vials of the three radiation-fight-
ing pills the computer had recommended and popped a few
into his mouth, swallowing them down with water from a
nearby faucet.

Taking as many of the boxes as he could carry, but leaving at least a little for the future, if there was any such thing,
Stone headed back out to the garage section and loaded them
up on top of the back of the Harley, securing them in place
on thick, nearly impervious plastic alloy boxes that sat in a
wide frame on the back of the motorcycle. Then he headed
back to the ammunition room and reloaded the Uzi 9-mm
auto-pistol. He had felt naked without it. But an extra batch
of thirty- and fifty-round clips, and four dozen magazines
for the Ruger .44, made him just a little more secure. He
loaded up his arms with more of the .89-mm Luchaire mini-
missiles. He had used them all up. What had seemed like a
lifetime supply when he had put the last batch on the bike

had gone in under a month. Now he would hoard them like diamonds. He carried a half dozen out to the Harley, snapping them in place in a slim-line auto-feed built on the side of the bike so he could pop each shell up and slam it right into the tubular launcher.

Stone made a final trip back to where he knew the pitbull would be waiting. Still, he wasn't quite prepared for the mess it had managed to make in the hour they had been there. The canine had somehow pushed the chair over to the kitchen cabinets where it knew cans of food were stored, had managed to climb up on said chair, open the cabinet doors, knock out rows of the carefully stacked tins of everything from sardines to toothpaste, ravioli to apricots in syrup. Not that the terrier knew what the hell it was doing. But as every oak tree knows—from the littlest acorn . . . Thus some of what crashed to the ground the fighting cannonball of muscle and leathery hide found appetizing. In fact, it found a surprising variety—and quantity—of the mixed together substance to be to its liking.

"Oh, God, dog," Stone whispered, his face growing pale as he saw the damage the creature had inflicted on his mother's once clean kitchen. She would be turning in her grave. Stone had a sudden vision of her, back when they had all lived together, of how she had yelled at him for leaving a plate of chicken out at night, saying it would bring in the bugs and the rats. If she could only see it now. The thought brought a smile to his face.

"Come on, dog, you're going to pay for this, when I can figure out how." Stone said as he leaned over and threw a handful of the anti-radiation drugs into the pitbull's mouth. The animal gulped, burped, farted, and then swallowed them down along with a final mouthful of some sort of reddish liquid it had been slurping out of a half-chewed can. Casting a final eye around to see if it had somehow missed any particularly delectable goodies, the canine decided it had used up this scene. And with a snort, as if to indicate the party was over because *it* was leaving, the pitbull turned on its heels and walked after Stone, its somewhat enlarged stomach rolling from side to side, almost scraping the floor like the gondola of a blimp in rough winds.

Once they were outside of the bunker again, Stone watched with a sense of dread as the granite doors closed behind him, moving smoothly on the huge ball bearings that his father had had installed. The kind used to move the rockets down at the Cape. When there had been such things. He always felt like it would be the last time he saw the place each time he left it. The world seemed to be getting more dangerous by the day. Stone returned the radio transmitter to the ground, wrapping it back inside the thick plastic, and rolled the boulder over it. Excaliber looked at him with intrigued eyes, wondering what sort of bone it was that needed such a large rock over it.

Stone checked his luminescent watch dial, turning his wrist up, and saw that there was just enough time to get back to the bivouac before dawn. The sky looked solid as a rock now, just one immense cloud that was heading south a few miles an hour faster than it had been before. But it was staying high for the moment. He couldn't smell any rain. Rain that would bring the poison back down to earth.

They shot along the dirt path at a fast clip, and Stone felt kind of reckless at this point. It sure as hell wasn't like his life expectancy was going up or anything. He kept trying to tell himself that he didn't have rad poisoning. But the more he denied it, the more it clawed at his mind, at his thoughts. Like an itch he didn't want to scratch, the very denial of its existence gave it increased power to grab him. He *did* feel hot everywhere. He *could* feel cold sores coming out on his mouth. His brain *did* feel like it was warmed-over Jell-O. On the other hand, he hadn't slept for about fifty hours, either. That might have something to do with it. Yeah, he was sleepy, that was all. And if he was incredibly lucky and made it back to camp as fast as he had left it, he might even be able to get a nice long sleep of about forty-five minutes or so.

Excaliber sensed it first. In a flash he was up on the backseat, his front paws up over Stone's shoulders, a motion that his master knew the animal only exhibited on threatening occasions. He loosed his jacket with one hand, freeing the Uzi for quick draw if he needed it. Then Stone heard

it—a drone like a mosquito, then a bee, getting louder by
the second. Suddenly he saw it—a light coming straight
toward them. But it seemed to be floating. As the beam
came to rest squarely on his face, nearly blinding him, Stone
realized it was a chopper. They were being hunted from the
air.

The whirring blades of the Mini Huey filled the sky over
Stone's head with a deafening roar, and the pitbull set to
barking up at the craft, which, even twenty yards up and
forty or so in front of them, sent a gale storm of wind down
at them, whipping the grit from the road into their eyes and
mouths. Above the Harley, which had skidded to a stop—
Stone couldn't see, could barely keep the big bike upright—
three men looked down from the mini-attack chopper
debating whether to try to take Martin Stone alive or shoot
him dead on the spot. Their boss had said either way was
fine. As long as his head was brought back—attached to its
body or not. They decided to kill him. From each side of the
chopper's bulbous plastic cockpit two hit-men opened up
with .45-caliber Ingrams, the preferred hit weapon, Stone
knew, of the Mafia death squads.

Two rows of slugs plowed straight toward the bike and its
occupants, sending up small violent eruptions of dust in the
exploding asphalt of the one-laner as they scissored their
way inexorably forward.

"Jump," Stone screamed, leaping from the bike with
every ounce of strength in his tired legs. He felt the muscles
tighten, then uncoil—and he was flying through the air and
darkness. Everything around him was a screaming hell of
whistling slugs that he could feel tearing right by him, just
inches away from his face, his chest. His body flipped and
corkscrewed through the shadows and then came down hard
in some bushes. Stone felt the air get knocked out of him as
he landed, but he made himself go with it, not panicking,
and was able to absorb most of the blow. He spun around
from the darkness of the little grove of wild shrubs as the
chopper buzzed past, its scythes of .45-caliber steel leaving
a pockmocked, broken road behind.

Stone knew he had only seconds. Already the chopper
was turning around a hundred yards past and starting back.

This time they would hover over him and send down a fusillade. There was no way he could survive. He looked off behind him, hoping to find sheltering woods but saw only a long, sloped field of low bushes, a few cacti—no place to hide. Suddenly his head swung around to the Harley, on the road twenty feet ahead of him. He had rearmed the Luchaire back at the bunker. See, he wasn't such a stupid guy, after all. Getting to it, loading it, before the chopper reached him again, that was another...

Stone let his mind argue about the feasibility of such an action while his body took off leaping over the bushes on the run. He reached the bike just as he saw the chopper complete half its turn, about fifty feet up, the wide and blinding searchlight beneath the craft lighting a circular patch of terrain below with the sudden noonday illumination of the sun. Animals and lizards, caught in the light, froze like statues until the Huey was past, and then ran, terrified, back to their holes and lairs. Only Stone had nowhere to hide.

He fumbled at the autofeed of the magazine that was attached to the side of the Electraglide. His hands seemed to want to move by themselves, doing little fumbling dances at the release for the shells.

"Come on, you little assholes," Stone screamed down at his own fingers, demanding that they do what they were paid to. At last the thumb and forefinger of his right hand managed to get it together enough to click the lever—and up popped one of the long rockets. Stone grabbed it just as the light of the chopper began steering a path through the darkness back toward him. He ripped the release off the launching tube and pulled it out toward him, so the unit snapped out on steel hinges. Stone slammed the shell in and spun around alongside the firing cylinder. He slid back the "arm" signal and then turned to sight up the chopper.

Sighting it up was not exactly the problem. It wasn't like he couldn't find it, but that the damn thing was suddenly right there, looming toward him like some sort of flying pterodactyl of the Pleistocene Era searching for dinner. He couldn't see in the sudden blinding impact of the searchlight but could distinctly hear the snaps of the two Ingrams opening up on him again. Stone tried desperately to sight it but could see only the light—a sun of brilliance taking out his vision.

Stone aimed at the light itself, at its blinding center even as it filled the very air above him, and pulled the trigger. The tube at his side seemed to explode as the bike shook violently from side to side. Stone found himself thrown backward by a sudden roar of such power that he felt as if his very flesh were being shaken from his bones. He found himself suddenly sitting back on his ass, slamming down onto the hard roadway as his eyes snapped up straight ahead. The chopper, just fifty feet in front of him, was on fire. Within, Stone could see the hit men coated with flames, like marshmallows sizzling with blue licks of fire as they melt within a camp fire. Only these marshmallows were screaming. The horrible screams of those who perish by fire.

But they didn't have a hell of a long time to wait to die. The gas tanks of the chopper suddenly went, as the flames created by the detonation of the 89-mm spread into the fuel pumps. The secondary went up like Mt. Vesuvius in the sky, blasting the occupants and the craft itself out in all directions in a maelstrom of blazing particles. The ruins rained down for two hundred feet around, depositing flaming debris in numerous piles in the darkness. Suddenly there were hundreds of fires burning around the hillside, like some sort of sacrificial blazes. Fires to the gods. The dark gods. The death gods, who drank death, inhaled the smoke of burning things like the intoxicating vapors of the finest opium. The smoke of the dead men—and the smoking, smashed husk of the chopper—rose and mingled together, indistinguishable anymore as being man or machine. Rose higher and higher, as if reaching to join the great atomic clouds far above.

Chapter Six _____

S tone rose slowly after the main storm of the chopper debris had fallen back down to earth. Dancing particles filled the air, their crystalline shapes reflecting back little rays from the flames of the many fires below. That had been close, Stone thought with a rapidly beating heart. Too close. He looked down and saw that the front of his jacket was singed, his eyebrows and hair burned at the very edges.

Someone was after him bad, real bad. Enough to send out a fucking chopper, just to wait around in hiding—wait for Martin Stone to show up. And, of course, acting like a predictable mouse in a maze, Stone had done so. It felt great to be loved so much. He had made a lot of enemies in his short career out of the bunker, but somehow he hadn't quite realized he was already on the number-one shit list of the bad guys. Well, if nothing else, Stone thought with bitter humor, he must be doing something right.

He looked around, suddenly realizing the pitbull was nowhere in sight. But even as he strained to find it, the animal rose slowly from a muddy ditch across the one-lane road, covered with muck and dirt. Excaliber gave Stone a dirty look that he could feel even through the fiery shadows.

"I told you from the start dog," Stone said, looking the pitbull squarely in the eye. "When you travel with me, it's flak time all the time." The fighting dog looked somewhat chagrined by the turn of recent events. He had figured it was going to be bad—but this bad? A nice nuclear explosion before breakfast, a raiding party of mountain bandits after lunch, a chopper attack for a late-night snack. Excaliber shook himself violently for about five seconds, apparently trying to dislodge the blanket of debris that pretty much coated him at this point. Branches, dirt, little pieces of powdered helicopter flew off the vibrating animal like molecules being hurled free from a centrifuge.

Once the bullterrior had cleaned itself sufficiently so at least it didn't feel like a junkyard dog, it barked, gave Stone its usual look of amused resignation, and stood up on its back legs so its front paws were leaning against his chest. The narrow almost Oriental-looking face with its hooded, almond-shaped eyes loomed closer and closer, as if it were trying to make contact with his very soul. That was the thing he liked about animals, Stone thought with a chuckle as the canine's long sandpaper-like tongue flapped across its master's cheek—they forgot right away. Unlike human beings who could and usually did carry a grudge their whole life, the dog would let the anger, the feeling of betrayal, whatever it was, sweep through it, and then be gone. It wasn't that it didn't feel it but that it felt it *completely*. And then, like a cloud passing over the face of the sky, the darkness was gone and the animal's face brightened again, ready for life, ready for whatever would come.

"We could all learn a lot from you, you stinking ball of fur!" Stone laughed as the thick animal smell of the dog's coat and tongue seemed to fill his senses. Stone suddenly had the absurd image of animals teaching men—giving them lessons in how to act properly. How to feel things fully, then let them pass without holding on either to the hate or the desire. The road to enlightenment taught by dogs, cats, hogs . . .

"Come on, let's get out of here," Stone said, suddenly pushing the pitbull back off him, "before I completely lose my mind." He walked back over to the bike and saw that other than lying on its side and being covered with another coating of soot and small pieces of metal, it was all right. He lifted the 1200-cc with a burst of grunting and expletives. The thing weighed a ton. But after a few seconds it was up, and he mounted it, testing the wheels by bouncing up and down. Excaliber leapt up on the seat, Stone instant-started the engine, and they were off again, leaving the funeral fires behind to heat the cold night in waves of shimmering heat that rose up from the old country road.

Stone tore through the night as the aurora far above seemed to at last tire out a little and drop back to a dim, pulsing pattern. The sky farther above was black. Not a star, the moon, nothing piercing the veil. It was as dark on the plains as he had ever seen it, as if a blanket had been dropped over the world. But the tunnel of light from his "fog buster" filled the mountain roads that he shot up and down with a flood of light. The nocturnal predators and prey of the forests scampered wildly off from the commotion of the passage of the Harley. Stone could see the yellow pairs of eyes of other wolf packs here and there staring out from among the forest. But the smell of blood was thick on the wind. They had made their kill—and were satiated—for the moment. One of them let out a low howl from behind a grove of trees. But Excaliber returned the growl in the same spine-chilling tone of caged animal fury. The pitbull would let no other animal challenge it—without returning the challenge.

Stone didn't like being pursued. It was one thing to battle it out, it was another to have some asshole—rather, a whole group of assholes—spending their every living day doing nothing but trying to kill you. A shiver ran down his back. Mafia? Guardians of Hell? The Dwarf? No, *he* was dead. Stone had killed him with his own hands. Not that it really mattered. They were all so interconnected, using one another for their own sick purposes. But someone, someone big, had obviously taken an extra-special interest in him. Death was carrying his name tag these days. The sky above looked like the lid of a coffin that was about to close forever.

Stone was able to make good time and soon was on part of an Interstate that took him within miles of the bivouac—if his compass and landmark reckonings were correct. They were. For suddenly he recognized some low peaks and turned off through a series of fields, covered with the dead brown husks of millions of mountain flowers that felt like a cushion beneath the thick wheels of the Harley.

Then he was at the camp, leaning down almost flat forward as he shot up the least angled slope of the thirty-foot-high plateau that sat like a little island of dirt rising up arrogantly from the bushy terrain around it. The second he reached the camp and the bike leveled out, Stone saw there was trouble. Big trouble.

Leaping Elk and Meyra were facing each other in a cleared space, a dirt circle about fifteen feet wide. They were just a yard or so apart, and Stone saw with horror as a vagrant ray of crackling light from the fire danced along them that they were holding razor-sharp Cheyenne hunting knives in their hands. There wasn't a sound in the camp, just Leaping Elk's sickening smile as he stared at the much smaller Indian woman and the spreading circle of red on her buckskin jacket.

Stone brought the Harley to a screeching halt, leaping from the big motorcycle so fast that it didn't have time to release its auto kickstand and the whole machine tumbled over into the dirt, skidding sideways for about ten feet. Excaliber, who had just been waking himself from his usual traveling nap, barely had time to open his eyes before he found himself hurtling through the air and into the narrow branches of a nearby low tree. The dog groaned and curled itself up into a ball before it made contact. This was getting ridiculous, Excaliber thought angrily just before he struck. He was going to have to have a long, long talk with his master, who, he was now seeing, for all the food he provided—and that wasn't a hell of a lot now that the pitbull thought about it—seemed to have a knack for producing painful experiences for the dog to go through. But it didn't have a hell of a lot of time to dwell on the subject as the tree suddenly got real close.

Stone ran across the plateau as fast as his legs could carry him, moving in a dark blur so that he suddenly crashed through the crowd of Indians and his own NAA recruits, who were all looking at the whole thing like it was some sort of late-night TV amusement. Stone started forward toward Leaping Elk, who still hadn't realized Stone had returned and was locked in mortal combat with Meyra, who circled slowly around him now, her legs low and crouched. Arms reached out from both sides of him, holding Stone back from running into the circle.

"No, you cannot," one of the younger braves whom Stone recognized as Shining Eagle, said, holding him firmly. "They must fight it out. It is the Cheyenne way. We must have a leader. And there is no other method of deciding."

"But she—she's just a woman," Stone half screamed as he saw Meyra suddenly glance over and realize that he was there. She looked startled, first a mixture of fear, then relief, as she saw who it was. Then suddenly fear again, as she realized she had let her guard down. Leaping Elk, all six-feet-four of him, suddenly moved forward like a charging bull, his long blade slashing out at her.

"She demanded it," Shining Eagle said. "She was the one who demanded the Trial of Knives. They must be allowed to—" But Stone wasn't listening. Not when the Cheyenne woman was about to join her ancestors in a hurry.

"Fuck that shit," Stone spat out with the simple but eloquent words of someone who wasn't about to be stopped. He gripped both of his hands together and in a flash slammed back and forth with his elbows into the faces of each of the Cheyenne braves, who staggered backward in a total daze. Bringing his arms forward with the reverse motion, Stone used the energy to launch himself ahead so that he shot forward the twelve feet separating the battling Cheyenne from himself like a projectile. Even as Stone moved, his mind thinking at lightning speed, he calculated in millisecond computerlike debate whether to reach for his pistol or knife, which were equidistant from his right hand, since he would be upon the fight by the time he got either of them out.

In a quarter second Stone decided to go for the knife, and his hand snapped down toward the hilt, gripping it hard. By a half second he had it coming out and up in a tight arc. Then everything speeded up like a film coming loose from its sprockets. At the last second Leaping Elk, whose blade was almost at Meyra's throat, somehow sensed Stone coming. His attention was pulled around as he slackened his attack for a second. That was Meyra's opening. With the speed and power she had learned first from her father, one of the finest Cheyenne fighters in the territory, and later from her brother, the indian woman, barely twenty years old, snapped her right leg up with all her strength.

Leaping Elk took the kick full in the stomach and it sent him flying backward so he careened right past Stone, who didn't have time to react either. The Indian somehow caught himself from falling and came to a stop about three yards back. He sneered at Stone.

"You. You think you can get me? You're a fool." The Indian laughed that crazy laugh again. And Stone saw that the foam around his mouth had increased so that it now covered his lips completely. His radioactive hand, the one not holding the hunting blade, was nothing but a dripping mass now, a gelatinous blob of red and purple that no longer even had fingers or much of anything except a bulbous shape, with pus that oozed out and fell from scores of grape-sized boils.

"You can walk away," Stone said as he let his knees relax and sink and, slowly, as if hardly moving, began angling himself to prepare for the brave's attack. "And I won't follow. Just walk, man—walk *now*!"

"Walk?" The Cheyenne laughed again, and blood began streaming from his nose, mixing with the white foam like shaving cream around his jaws. "Why walk when I have the magic hand?" The brave laughed again. Every time he laughed now, it seemed to send a little geyser of blood out of his nose, or his ears, or some part of his being. It was as if the body was actually decomposing from within, the radio-cative poisons he had breathed in, eaten, burned into himself had gone to work with a vengeance. He was dissolving inside, just a dammed-up wall of blood and cancerous cells ready to burst.

"The magic hand!" The Cheyenne laughed again. He held the diseased, rotting stump-claw up and waved it at Stone. Little pockets of slime and red and brown liquid glistened in the flickering rays of the fire as they sprayed into the air. Stone jumped back, as fast as a jackrabbit. He sure as hell didn't want to get any of that radioactive stew on him. He had just decided to reach for his gun, now that he was slightly out of range, when Leaping Elk charged with such speed that Stone was taken by surprise. He stopped his motion in midair and, realizing he didn't have time to regain his balance, fell down backward just as the Indian's knife hand descended from the sky like the cleaving sword of the great Cheyenne war gods.

The blade passed less than an inch away from Stone's left shoulder, but Stone, as he fell to the ground, slammed the point of his fourteen-inch Randall custom bowie straight into the Indian's chest. The knife went in sideways, slipping between two ribs right at the top of the rib cage. Stone slid the length of the Cheyenne's chest, letting the full weight of his own body falling bring the knife straight down. Like a butcher's cleaver, the long hunting blade cut straight down and through the chest and stomach, splitting the entire midsection of the Cheyenne open like a gutted steer. The heart, intestines, organs, every damn thing that pumped and churned away inside the Indian's body, exploded out as if shot from a slingshot. The fleshy debris filled the air in a tornado of red.

Stone ripped the knife out as it reached the Cheyenne's pelvic bone and continued his own fall so that as the exploding body organs erupted forward, he was going in the opposite direction. He rolled along the ground in a tight ball. When he came up to his feet and spun around, the Indian had already fallen straight forward, stretched out full-length. He lay motionless in the garbage dump of his own organs, heart sliced in two, each side still desperately pumping away like a fish out of water, though nothing was sucked into their gasping ventricles but red dirt.

Chapter Seven _____

As Stone walked carefully around the spreading swamp of body organs, the rest of the audience looked at him like he was the last actor left in a Shakespearean tragedy in which everyone else had just been killed. Their eyes were filled with an equal mixture of amazement, anger, relief, fear—every goddamn emotion know to men.

Stone didn't pay them any heed once he saw that no one else was going to launch himself at him—at least for a second or two. He made his way around the butchered corpse and over to Meyra, who was just starting to rise from the ground. She had her hand over her right breast, and a scarlet stain had spread out nearly six inches in diameter right through her buckskin jacket. But her eyes looked clear, and her face still had color in it as she rose.

"Are you all right?" Stone asked with concern as she stumbled for a second, holding on to his arms for support.

"Yes. Yes—I think so." The Cheyenne woman gave a frightened smile at the man who had just saved her life. "Thank you, Martin Stone. Whether or not you should have interfered," she said softly, "I don't know. But I do know I would have been dead in a few seconds at most. I don't want to die. So thank you. Though I know it was my fault to demand the Challenge of the Knives. But after you left, after his balls pulled themselves back into place, he came back out from his hole and started bothering everyone again, waving that horrible hand around. I couldn't stand it, I just couldn't. No one else would do anything."

"It's all right. It had to be done," Stone said, comforting her and holding her shoulder in his hand. "The man wasn't just a bastard—he also had radiation poisoning. It can drive men to complete madness before it actually kills them. Then they must be destroyed like rabid dogs." Stone turned toward the nervous men. They all looked uptight. The Indians because Stone had apparently just broken a sacred Cheyenne rule—and because they seemed to have quite unsettled feelings about allowing a woman to lead them now. Stone's own NAA men—Bull and the three other young recruits— looked concerned about the Cheyenne, who glared at them now, their ever present but usually hidden deep mistrust of the white man broken through in near vengeful fury. Though they had all hated Leaping Elk, they hated Stone, a white man, having killed him, even more. It stirred something primitive in their hearts. The white race, after all, had not been too generous in its near annihilation of the various American tribes.

The whole damned scene was degenerating rapidly. Stone could see that if nothing else. And he realized for the hundredth time why he hated this leadership bullshit. Things had been at least less complicated, if no less dangerous, when it had just been him and the dog.

"Look," Stone said at last after nearly twenty seconds of complete silence by the entire force as they all tried to gauge each other's intentions. "I know there's a lot to talk about and that I may have broken your tribal regulations, but give me a break, okay? I'm exhausted. I haven't slept now for four days. Even if we dissolve this whole damn unit in a few hours—just let me get two or three hours of some fucking shut-eye, okay? 'Cause I feel like a dead man right now. Can hardly even focus." Stone tried to make his right eye sort of close and start twitching—for credibility's sake—though he didn't have to try very hard.

The Cheyenne looked at one another and mumbled a few remarks. Then one of them turned back.

"All right, Stone. You've got your few hours. Let's say until the sun has risen to the branches of that tree." He

pointed to the low wooden fingertips of a large fir some
thirty yards off. Stone gauged that would happen at about
nine in the morning. It was four-thirty now. That was almost
five hours. Good God, he'd feel like he'd been to Club Med.

"But then we talk. We decide things once and for all," the
brave went on coldly. The Indians stared at Stone hard, as
did all the others. As glad as he'd been that they'd fought on
his side for the last week, Stone suddenly felt equally appre-
hensive if they should turn against him. They moved forward, and Stone almost felt himself reaching for his Uzi as
beads of sweat started to roll down his forehead. But they
stopped after a few yards and began gathering the parts of
their recently deceased tribal brother.

He should have an uncle in the funeral business, Stone
thought with dark bitterness. All this killing, it didn't
make a guy feel too good. And yet Stone had the gift for
death, for dispensing death. The Nadi was the name given
him by a tribe of Ute Indians who had saved him when he
and his family had first emerged from the bunker after his
father's heart attack. It had been Stone's idea to come out.
Great idea. The Winnebago they had stocked as if going
on a little picnic had hardly gotten a few hours from the
bunker when they'd been attacked by a roving band of
Guardians of Hell bikers out for some fun. His mother had
been savagely raped and mutilated, his sister kidnapped,
and Stone himself beaten and kicked to within an inch of
his life. Less than an inch.

"Nadi," Stone mumbled under his breath. "Nadi, Nadi."

"What was that?" Meyra asked, turning to him so the
whole side of her body was pressing against him. He could
still feel her flesh quivering as if she was freezing.

"Nothing," Stone said with a deep sigh, looking up at the
sky to try to grasp hold of the stars, the moon, for a second,
to find his bearings. But there was only that black sheet high
above, the spreading cloud of atomic death that seemed to
gather in the darkness and swell as it spread out across Colorado to the east and south. He almost felt tears come to his
eyes. It was as if there were nothing sometimes. Just an
abyss into which one could fall if one looked too long,
thought about it too often. Everything was wounded or dead;

even the sky was filled with a black blood that would soon rain down. The abyss. It never had seemed closer.

"Come on," Meyra said suddenly. "You look like shit. Come with me. I need your help, anyway." He started along, almost dragged by the young Cheyenne woman hardly half his size. Stone caught Bull's eye as he was led in a near daze away from the fire and toward Meyra's all-terrain vehicle, parked near a boulder in the darkness.

"Keep an eye on things, okay, man?" Stone whispered through the flame-stitched darkness out of the corner of his mouth as if he were trying to be a ventriloquist.

"Sure, Stone. Get some sleep. We'll cover your back," Bull replied, giving the thumbs-up. He immediately headed back to the tank where he set himself down in the fold-out metal seat, just a few feet below the top of the hatchway, and sat there putting his legs up out of the hatch and crossing his arms. Like a watchman at a proverbial factory, the big ex-NAA recruit watched the scene below him with a wary eye.

"Here," Meyra said as she knelt down and crawled into the little lean-to that she had created by putting a large blanket between the three-wheeler and a six-foot-high, egg-shaped boulder. "My little home." Stone followed behind her, closing the flap, and with the lantern she suddenly snapped on and the pads of blankets on the ground, it did feel like a goddamn home. More of one than he'd had for a long time.

"Just lie back," she said with an almost imperceptible little smile that dashed back and forth across her full lips. She reached over and gently pushed him back so he lay down on a thick bearskin pelt that felt exquisitely wonderful and soft against his aching back and legs. He let his head fall back onto a hide pillow and closed his eyes, suddenly deciding that maybe things weren't that bad, after all. And when he opened them again just a slit a few seconds later, he saw that things were a hell of a lot better than he could have imagined.

Meyra was just pulling off her olive sweatshirt beneath her buckskin so that her full, young, pear-shaped breasts bounced out into the rippling rays of the erratic light put out by the short-circuiting lamp off to one side of the little shelter. His eyes suddenly opened wide and his heart started beating faster. Stone wondered if sleep was as close as it had seemed a second ago.

Naked from the waist up, she examined herself in the thin rays of illumination. Leaping Elk had gotten her right breast —one good slice along the outer side, about three inches long. She held her breast in her hands, pushing it up and toward her to get a good look at the wound. The blood was still oozing out, but it wasn't spurting or flowing fast. As deep as it had gone, the wound hadn't severed any large veins or dug into an artery. She would live. The Cheyenne woman reached into a bison-hide pouch attached to her belt and extracted a small piece of hollow mountain-goat horn, sealed at both ends. She took off a bark cap and poured about a tablespoon full of green powder into her hand. Carefully recapping the horn, she grabbed some water from a nearby gourd and sprinkled just enough into the powder to make it into a paste. Meyra dug the fingers of her other hand into the stuff, mixing it around for nearly a minute until it was of a thick oatmeal consistency. She slopped the goo-filled hand down on her breast and smeared the green stuff all over the wound, even opening it and pressing the paste inside.

Stone alternately opened and closed his eyes at the scene. Though he liked looking at her breast, he didn't necessarily like the vision of her pushing green slime onto it. She caught him staring at her suddenly, and she let out a sharp little laugh.

"You look funny," she said with smile. "You have a very strange expression on your face."

"Yeah, well, I don't get to see swamp juice pumped into a beautiful breast too often," Stone replied in a low and tired voice.

"Cheyenne medicine," Meyra said as she looked back down at her right breast to make sure she was getting every square inch saturated with the not-unpleasant-smelling slop. "My father was a medicine man, besides being chief of our tribe. He showed me and—and Little Bear all the secrets of herbal healing. The Spirit Gods have given mankind everything he needs on this earth to heal and protect his body. But no one ever listened to the stupid Indian. They had more fun making pills and injections of powerful drugs that most of the time they didn't even know the results of, the long-term impact. All that I use on my body—and the others of the tribe—are natural things, given from nature, from the plants and the seeds, the minerals of the ground. I am the Healer now. It is all here, Stone. All. Everything has been provided. It takes a scientist not to know it."

"I'm not going to argue." Stone laughed, wanting to reach up and cup those golden breasts more every second. "You saved my ass just recently with a similar type of goo, if my memory serves me correct."

"That's right, *gringo*," she said, finishing up with her treatment. She didn't bandage the wound or anything, although already the paste seemed to be drying up and forming a shiny, protective coating. Blood was no longer flowing. "I saved your ass, and now you saved mine." And as if all the talk of "asses" made her physical embodiment of such an attribute want to get in on the action, Meyra suddenly stripped off her jeans and was stark naked before Stone, her perfect, lithe body, glistening with a thin coat of sweat that seemed to sparkle like diamonds in the low light.

Stone's hands suddenly reached out as if with minds of their own. He grabbed her around the ass, pulling her down on top of him. She fell, half squealing, half laughing, and suddenly she was crushing hard against him, pulled toward his chest by his strong arms, though he was careful to keep her right breast just off him so as not to open the wound again.

"Zounds," she said with another little laugh that sent shivers through Stone's back. "Me thought you were near gone from this world, into the land of Nod." Her face was so beautiful to him as it glowed from the lantern's stroking rays, smiling, eyes open and there for him, without a trace of darkness or deceit behind the shining brown irises. Her body was a soft paradise of flesh covering him. A musky perfume, sweet and filled with both the scents of flowers and animals in heat, seemed to drift from her entire body, intoxicating Stone, making him swoon, making his nasal passages open up, his lungs fill with the scent like an opium he had to inhale.

Suddenly her face came down close to his and she pressed her lips against his. For a few seconds she bobbed up and down on him with her mouth, like a timid bird testing a bite of food. And then suddenly her mouth was glued to his, and her tongue was seeking a desperate entry. They kissed hard, and Stone pulled her even tighter against him, loving the way she felt, the way she cleaved to him like a glove around a hand. Suddenly she seemed to jerk, and Stone groaned loudly as he felt the golden triangle between her legs become hot and burning with desire.

"Here," she said simply, suddenly rising up and away from him. "You are tired, let me disrobe you, as the woman should." She kneeled around him as he lay flat on his back on the bear rug and she peeled off first his pants, then his jacket and shirt, until he was as naked as she was. She looked down admiringly at him, her lips filling with desire. In the little bit of light that was still being emitted from the half-working lantern, she could see his recent scars, wounds over myriad parts of his body that he had been collecting from various delightful experiences over the last few months.

"You've been hurt," she said, kneeling back down by his side and stroking a long purple streak than ran down the whole side of his ribs, as if someone had almost, but not quite, driven a knife into him and skewered him as he had just done to Leaping Elk.

"Nothing fatal." Stone grinned as he felt his manhood rising for her as a tree rises for the sun. "Anyway, my uncle's a plastic surgeon out in Beverly Hills—said he could fix all gunshot, stabbing, and razor wounds—at twenty percent off—since I'm a relative. Have to get out that way—as soon as I can move, of course."

"You're crazy." She laughed again, with a wide-eyed kind of girlish innocence in her face that all women get when they're with a man they know they could love. "Hold my breasts," she said to him in a guttural whisper. "Hold them, squeeze them." Stone didn't need much coaxing in that department and reached up, cupping her round breasts, which were now as hard as freshly plucked fruits, the dime-sized nipples rising up for his mouth. Stone squeezed her, softly at first, rolling his hands around the Cheyenne woman's flesh. And then, as she groaned, he squeezed harder, kneading her hot mounds in his hands and fingers with an animal intensity. He felt her lips twitch against him, and her whole body seemed to soften and relax as she gave in to his maleness, his possession of her.

"My right breast, massage it," she said, commanding him urgently.

"But won't it hurt—" Stone began to protest.

"Touch heals all wounds, especially the touch of a man and a woman. Especially your touch. Your touch will heal me. Like magnets—that's what we're like. Like magnets." She groaned again as his organ stiffened more and throbbed up against her thighs like something alive. Suddenly she could stand it no more. She wanted him, needed him. His staff, the magic wand that healed all wounds. She lowered herself down in front of him until her head was at his groin. She buried her face in his dark hair, rolling it around as if in a luxurious fabric. With both hands she gripped the stiff organ that curved upward into the air like a sword of flesh. And then, as if in a mesmerized state, she lowered her mouth down over it.

Stone moaned in the darkness now as but a few orange rays trickled out from the now virtually dead battery lamp. She moved up and down, a little farther each time, and her long black hair cascaded down over his stomach like a curtain of silk. She seemed to take him down impossibly deep, opening her throat, her lips, wide. But her desire drove her to that extra madness that super horniness brings out, and she drove herself down on his stiff organ as if she had to get it all inside her or die.

Stone nearly screamed out as he felt her lips and throat suddenly push down, covering him completely. He was totally enveloped in the velvet warmth of her throat. He pumped involuntarily into her, knowing he was pushing deep, but she grunted and just took him even farther, her hands now around his testicles, squeezing them hard as she fed his manhood into her mouth.

Suddenly it was Stone who couldn't stand it anymore, and he pulled her up from her kneeling position so that his staff ripped out of her mouth, a coating of saliva from stem to top. With the strength of total arousal he literally lifted her up above his midsection and then lowered her down atop him. She pulled her legs apart as she came down on him, reaching down to make a path through the wet, furred forest of reddish-golden hair that formed a triangle between her legs. They stared into each other's eyes, seeing each with only the dim light from the camp-fire that percolated beneath the edges of the lean-to. Their eyes were locked in electric circuitry as his organ suddenly entered her.

He had barely pressed past her throbbing opening when Stone felt a shudder of raw energy pass through him. Holding her tight around the waist, he pulled down with all his might as he thrust up into her. The entire organ entered the beautiful Cheyenne warrior woman in a second, stunning her with its thickness and length. Kneeling atop him, her eyes seemed to close tight as her whole head fell to one side, so powerful was the sensation of being filled with him.

Stone relaxed for a second, barely gaining control of himself. Then, pulling himself back down into the bearskin, he moved his hands down and gripped her around the ass and the top of her thighs. Slowly he pushed up into her, then out again. And slowly her mind returned to her, though she began breathing hard as she followed his strokes. Moving with him, her pelvis rotating around on the organ, her arms, leaning down on his chest, pressing up and down as she did push-ups on him.

Then she seemed to go completely crazy as she suddenly began pumping up and down on him like a pneumatic jackhammer. She would raise herself up until the very tip of him was in her and then come down hard, all the way to the hilt, so that her buttocks were slamming right against his stomach. Faster she went, moving with total abandon as her mouth fell open and drool trickled slightly from both corners. Drool from the food of the body. Stone could hardly hang on as she rocketed up and down atop him.

Then they were both driving hard against each other, their bodies slamming together in loud, wet sounds as their desire came to a fevered pitch. Then they were both animals, inhuman creatures whose flesh and smell were the only realities, the only consciousness. Both in the state of highest bliss a man and a woman can know on this fucked-up planet, they ground their bodies like savage beasts as Stone pumped a lava of love into her volcanic center.

Chapter Eight _____

W hen Stone awoke, light was seeping in under the edge of the blanket—and a white-and-brown face along with it. Excaliber stood half in, half out, of the little lean-to, not positive he was welcome. But as soon as Stone's eyes opened and the pitbull made eye contact with his master, he pushed forward off his powerful back legs and in a second was on top of Stone and Meyra, a pile of legs that walked over their flesh with cold paws.

"What the hell"—the Cheyenne woman sputtered as she woke up, a paw digging into her right ear—"is going on?" She pushed away at the ghostly presence with both hands and sat up.

"Off, Excaliber, off!" Stone commanded the pitbull with a mean tone in his voice. The animal jumped off and slinked toward the flap, head down, emitting a pitiful little whine.

"Ah, he feels bad," Meyra cooed with the sudden concern of her latent maternal instincts. As if the dog heard her, it turned around, looking at them both with a pathetic, plaintive expression worthy of Bambi.

"Here, pooch, here," she said, clapping her hands.

"You're making a mistake," Stone began. "That animal's the biggest con artist alive. He can get food from a starving orphan." But it was too late, the bullterrier was already upon them with happy, slurping kisses all over the place.

By the time they got everything sorted out and emerged from the blanket shelter with shit-eating grins that only those who have been fucking all night can have, the rest of the fighting unit were already gathered around the cooking fire, which had been built up again so that it stood several feet high with crisscrossed, burning dead branches. The warming flames felt good in the cool, dark morning air as Stone made his way, rubbing his eyes, half stumbling toward the flames and the beckoning scent of coffee cooking up in several pots over the fire.

He and Meyra sat down without a word and poured themselves cups. They took a few sips and then looked up simultaneously. The eyes of the entire group were upon them.

"We were talking," one of the braves, Singing Crow, said to be so named, if Stone remembered correctly, for his soulful renditions of tribal songs performed for the Cheyenne as they traveled through the badlands together.

"And?" Stone grunted as he took a deep gulp of the burning black liquid, nearly scalding the back of his throat as he did so. He was still bone-tired. He wondered why.

"And," Singing Crow went on, "we worked a few things out. After you two—eh—retired," the young Cheyenne said diplomatically, for the sounds of the two in passion had occasionally drifted across the camp during the course of the night, "we started trying to sort things out."

"This didn't hurt." Bull grinned from the other side of the fire, holding up an empty bottle of gin that had miraculously appeared from out of the woodwork.

"Yeah," the Cheyenne went on. "We partook of the peace pipe, liquid-style. And we talked like men. Not as Indian or white men but just men. And we found out that basically we're coming from the same place. Don't know where the hell we're going exactly. But know that at least in many ways we see things through the same shit-colored glasses."

"And we sure kick ass good when we work together," Bull spoke up from his side of the fire. "Your general strategy really seems to work, Stone," he said admiringly as the addressee tried to pry his eyelids apart. They felt like they were shut with glue. He took another huge swig of the thick but vaguely coffeelike substance and peered toward the pot to see if there was more.

"With the tank as the main core of protective firepower,"
Bull went on, his big farmer's face growing alive with enthusiasm, his eyes dancing, "and the all-terrains as a fast-
strike mobile force, we've been knocking all comers down
like they was pickup sticks looking to take a fall."

"You sound like a military man"—Stone laughed—"with
your 'protective firepower,' and 'fast-strike mobile force.'"

"Well, being a tank commander, it kind of gets you thinking, you know." Bull waxed poetic with a wistful look in his
brown eyes. "It's a lot of power—you got men under your
command and you're responsible for their lives. So I done a
little reading, on my own. Some manuals on tank warfare I
found inside the tank."

"Very commendable," Stone said with only a hint of sarcasm in his voice. He finished off his cup of now cold brew
and reached for the pot, again filling his cup to the top. He
needed two cups just to get the guts to look up at the sky that
morning, which he knew by the gray light that filtered down
between the men, by the dark peculiar mist in the air, by the
fire, almost soggy as it snapped hard to keep burning, was
bad. All he wanted to do was grab Meyra and head back to
the tent. Tell them to wake them in the spring, at the end of
hibernation.

"So we all talked, and we talked some more," Singing
Crow went on as the others looked on a little bleary-eyed but
nonetheless in good moods. "And we decided that maybe we
should stick together—for the moment, you know—"

"Yeah, for the moment," Bull spoke up, as did the others.
As if it had to be known by all that it was just a momentary
alliance that had been cemented largely by booze, and that
even in their half-drunk states they knew it could all unravel
like rotting twine at any moment.

"But the fact is," Singing Crow continued, "we all know
what it's like out there. In small numbers anyone is a target.
Even the tank—by itself—could be brought down with pet-
rol bombs." The Cheyenne spoke with great animation,
sweeping his arms around at his tribe, pointing. As he talked
excitedly, his black hair cascaded down from beneath the
baseball cap he had been wearing. The thick black mane fell
down both sides of his head and onto his shoulders. And

suddenly he looked, for all his well-made leather clothes and boots—like an Indian of centuries before, primitive, fierce, with a face forged from a life of steel-hard survival.

"*We*," the Cheyenne continued, "can be vulnerable to heavy firepower—that the tank can take out. It only makes sense. If together we can be ten times stronger, then for survival's sake alone we must unite our forces. Again—for the moment."

"Yes, of course." Stone smirked. "For the moment."

"And you're the elected chief, kemo sabe," the Cheyenne went on with a little twisted smile. You're the only one we could all even come near agreeing on to run the show. But you've gotten us through some pretty heavy shit already, and—"

"Look, fellahs, I appreciate the gesture and all that," Stone said, spitting out a huge twig from his coffee. "But I had been pretty much going to call it quits today and—" Even as he spoke, Stone suddenly saw that the unity was important to these men. That for the first time since the entire country had fallen into barbarism, things weren't still breaking down continuously into smaller and more primitive units as civilization itself headed backward in time like a roller coaster going the wrong way on the express track to hell.

Now two groups of men had joined together. Two unfathomably different cultures, ways of life. Years, centuries, of hate. Yet they were all Americans. Americans on the side of survival, life. Against those who carried the disease of death. The crime lords and the bikers, the cannibal kings, the rapists and mutilators. All of the slime out there that was trying to drag mankind into a pit it would never rise from again. At least those seated around the fire knew that whatever else, they were against that. And in a world of existential blood and nothingness that common bond was worth a lot.

"Look" Stone said, suddenly sitting up straight as he realized that their little drunken encounter group of participatory democracy had been an important moment. Suddenly he almost dared feel in a good mood. A much better mood than he had had the glimmerings of in a long, long time. Maybe there was hope for the fucking country, after all.

"Maybe there is something you could do. The people downwind of here are all going to die unless they take . . . these." He pulled out a canister of the pills from inside his jacket. "Here," he said, passing it around. "Take one red, one blue, and one green. You'll get your own batches to take."

"What the hell is that shit?" Singing Crow asked as he took the vial from Stone's outstretched hand.

"Potassium iodide is one, and the others . . . shit, I don't know what their names are, but they've been found to be able to almost completely fill the body's needs for a large number of minerals and trace elements, so the lungs, blood, and digestive system don't absorb any radiation from atomic particles or by-products of the bomb containing those elements."

"You really believe all that stuff?" Singing Crow asked, looking intensely at Stone.

"Yeah, I do," Stone replied. "Maybe I'm an asshole, and that's certainly a possibility, but I'm taking them myself. I'm going to keep taking them for at least a month—and I'm feeding them to my damn dog as well." As if offering a dramatic effect, the pitbull suddenly appeared from around a log and beelined toward an unattended cup of coffee, which he proceeded to slop up gustily. The entire fighting unit burst into laughter and seemed to relax appreciably. Stone knew why he had the mutt on salary.

Singing Crow looked defiantly around at his own people, then took out the three pills and downed them with a swig of coffee. He handed the vial to the next man and the next. Everyone took them except one—Fat Possum, the brave who had been Leaping Elk's lackey. Though his master was dead now, the basically stupid Indian somehow felt he had to keep the tradition of stupidity inspired by the late Elk going, even after he was gone. Thus, though he had been triply exposed to radiation as he had breathed in the radioactive particles, drank water right after the bomb, and eaten of the high-rad snakedogs, all in imitation of the dear departed, he didn't take the lifesaving pills.

His choice, Stone thought, reminding himself to keep an eye on the man. There were going to be a lot more cases of radiation madness. Of that he was sure.

But the rest of the Cheyenne—and all of the NAA recruits, who, having recently been in the ranks of General Patton III's army, were used to taking whatever medicines were doled out—took their doses.

"All right, then, you want to do something that will really help the poor bastards who live two hundred miles within this blast zone?" They looked at him expectantly. "Then distribute these pills to them. Tell them to take them for one month. Not to drink any water that falls in the next week, and after that to only use spring water, not running water, for at least a month. And finally—not to eat any animal or plant life from this area for at least the next year."

They looked at him as if he were a little on the crazy side.

"People don't give up their food, their homes, so easily," Singing Crow went on. He seemed to have become the unofficial spokesman for the Cheyenne, and they nodded as he spoke.

"I know," Stone said, watching as Excaliber finished up the cup of coffee in about two seconds flat. The pitbull's head rose up like a periscope and swiveled around, trying to search out any errant cups of coffee or bits of food that had been left lying around "unguarded." "That's why most of the people—at least those downwind of here—are probably going to die," Stone continued. "But we can try. It's their only chance. Those that stay—I guarantee you—are doomed. And their children, if born alive, will be mutants, clawed things, blind, scaled, who will curdle their mothers' milk in their breasts. You all saw what happened to Leaping Elk. He went mad. His brain was melted by the stuff, his guts turned to blood suey. That's radiation, man—pure and simple."

It had been hard for the Cheyenne to really take seriously the idea of radioactivity—after all, it was something you couldn't see, taste, smell, touch. How could you even know

it was real and not just another of the white man's illusions?
But they had seen Leaping Elk. And more than that, they
trusted Stone. So they took the pills, popped them down,
each with a swig of coffee or water to carry the foul-tasting
U.S.-government-issue generic pills into their guts, where
the radiation demons were hiding, their atomic claws glowing in the darkness of tubes and capillaries.

Chapter Nine _____

"What do you mean *you're* not coming?" Singing Crow blurted out after they had all just agreed to carry out Stone's request to distribute the anti-rad pills to the south.

"I can't, man," Stone said as he finished drawing a list of the nos when it came to avoiding radiation poisoning. "My sister's in trouble. Bad trouble. If I don't get to her, she's dead. She's the last of my family. I have no choice." For the Indians, family was the strongest tie. They had nothing else. Thus they understood his need to go, to drop all other things.

"But I'll meet up with you," he said, handing them the radiation warning poster that he had written. "As you travel, write up copies of this and put them up everywhere. Give out the pills to the local town rulers, mayors, chiefs, whatever the fuck is out there. Tell them the whole truth. Then it's up to them what they do. A lot will die, but for those who listen to you, it will save them. You men could save thousands of lives, you understand me? Thousands."

The importance of their task did start to dawn on the combined strike force, and looks of pride slowly appeared on their faces. They were actually doing something. A hell of a lot more than anyone else in this whole barbarous country.

"I know that area well," Singing Crow said. "My father and I used to hunt there. There are about a dozen Indian settlements, an equal number of white towns. We can hit all of them in a few days. Travel fast."

"And remember," Stone added as he stood up, addressing the rest of them, who remained seated. "Listen to the words on those leaflets you'll be putting up. 'Cause I don't want to see any of you suckers die. You're good men. A lot better than most out there. This country needs all it can get like you. Use your common sense—and maybe you'll all actually get through this."

Stone went back to his Harley and unloaded the boxes of pills, handing them out in equal numbers to each man, so that a total of a thousand doses for about two weeks were at hand. It would have to do. It was all they had. Whoever got them first out there and was clever enough to take them would survive. The rest—

The sky began darkening as if turning to night, although it was not yet ten in the morning. Stone reluctantly zipped up his jacket and whistled for the pitbull to get his ass on board. Meyra walked over to him as the Cheyenne checked the ties on their threewheelers so their loads would not come apart on the bumpy journey south.

"I think I'll miss you," she said, standing just inches from him. She rose up on tiptoes, kissed him softly on the lips, then pulled back again so that just the lightest of touches was left behind on his mouth, like a flower petal rubbing across his skin, a piece of velvet flesh.

"Well, if there's anything that'll keep me going out there," he said with the edge of a smile as he nodded over at the slate-black sky to the north and east where he was about to head to try to track down April, "it will be the thought of your delicious body in my arms. It's an image a man can carry for the rest of his life, a carrot to lure him forward like some sort of dumb mule."

"That's how I like my men." She smiled slyly as she stepped back from the Harley, which suddenly roared to life like an uncaged mountain cat. "Dumb and able to fuck even when they're wounded."

"That's me to a *t*." Stone laughed, throwing his head back. "There, we've been computer-matched. See, I have to make it back. For a second date." She turned suddenly without another word, as she didn't want Stone or the others to see the moisture forming in her eyes again. She hated feeling vulnerable, her emotions out there for all the world to see. That she was in love and terrified. Terrified, not for herself but for the man she had to admit she was in love with. Terrified that she would never feel his body against hers, or his stiffness deep inside her, like the sword of King Arthur unlocking her deepest woman's secrets.

"Where is that damn dog?" Stone spat out as he spun his head around, trying to sight the pitbull. But even as he spoke the words, the canine appeared out of nowhere and, with a wild kind of leap, jumped over a pile of empty pill crates and onto the back of the Harley. He just made it, his front paws landing at the very back of the leather seat. But his back feet slammed into one of the higher empty boxes, and it went tumbling off. With a yelp of pain the bullterrier lunged forward with a second effort and managed to pull himself through sheer flailing motions up onto the seat. When he had finally settled down, he looked up at Stone who was staring at him shaking his head from side to side. The pitbull let out an almost inaudible whine and buried his head in the seat, gripping hard on both sides with his legs. It had not been his greatest effort.

Stone glanced around, searching for Meyra, but she had already walked off and wouldn't look back. He eased the big bike ahead and down off one of the declinations so they were both almost at a ninety-degree angle to the ground for a few seconds. Then the front wheel of the Harley caught the slow curve in the earth below, at the base of the rise, and they landed almost smoothly, the motorcycle suddenly shooting ahead as soon as both wheels made contact with the earth. Stone didn't look back, either. There were only tears in the past. God knew what in the future.

He headed due east, along a series of open fields with low slopes and not too bumpy a surface grade, so he made some good speed. The sky looked so bad, he didn't even want to look at it. But every few minutes, unable to help himself, he would glance up and take another peek. It wasn't even noon yet, but the day was as dark as the inside of a thundercloud. It was as if it were twilight, a polar twilight.

The swirling fallout clouds had smoothed out now, spreading into long, flattened rings of radioactive debris that looked miles thick as they twisted slowly off to the east and south. The cloud above felt as if a solid object had been hammered up overhead, a curtain of steel, a wall of solid black iron.

Stone could just see without the headlight of the bike, of which he'd just as soon save the power. There weren't any more supplies to replace those he had in the bunker. And already items were getting low in a few areas. He was going to have to get greedy. The days of using up every damn thing were over.

"Your hear that, dog?" he asked, half twisting his head around toward the pitbull. "We're going to have to be frugal with supplies from now on. F-R-U-G-A-L—do you understand what that means, dog? It means one biscuit when you might want two, one side of steak when three or four would have hit the spot. We're *all* going to have make sacrifices. You hear me, sacrifices!" But the animal either was sound asleep or was pretending to be, and thus not subject to the lectures of human beings.

After about an hour of driving, Stone saw more dead animals. A tribe of raccoons, about fifteen of them. All of them were burned hideously, their fur pelts scarred and pitted like a sofa that someone had used as an ashtray. Then a whole hillside of deer; the damn things must have been on the rise and caught by the blast waves of the bomb skimming over the highest tips of land as it sent out diminished but still deadly energy past its thirty- and forty-mile destruction circles. As he drew past the family of deer, Stone's guts rocked with nausea, for the still half-furred creatures were covered with brown blankets of roaches. Thousands of them. Tens of thousands, rushing over the corpse feasts, grabbing out little brown pincers of deer meat and then taking them back to their grubby little holes in the desert floor.

He gunned the bike, not wanting the things even to take note of him, though Stone was sure they were only after dead things. There seemed to be more and more bugs and roaches. He prayed they were just a localized phenomena and not yet another problem to worry about. If the roaches started growing as big as cats and added on wings and fangs, Stone was going to pack it in, he decided right then and there.

But soon there was far more to worry about than bugs. The black clouds above had thus far been high up, not yet beginning their descent to earth to release their store of radioactive poison. But as Stone moved further east, a whole portion of the sky suddenly seemed to start dropping fast, as if diving off from the rest. He could suddenly smell moisture in the air, dank and chemical-tasting. Excaliber sat up straight, eyes wide open. He growled hard, his muzzle just behind Stone's neck. A wind started blasting down from the heavens, and Stone did everything he could not to lose control of the Harley. Bushes, small trees, and cacti all blew far over on their sides, up and down the low foothills around which the Rocky Mountains loomed like the homes of the gods, the Himalayas of the North American continent.

The blackness seemed to descend on them like someone slowly decreasing the current of electricity to a light bulb until they could hardly see a thing. The feeling of being crushed by a huge weight was overwhelming. It was as if a mountain were descending, just a black line of writhing moisture that dropped yards per second, coming down on the earth like a press.

"We've gotta stop, pal," Stone suddenly screamed out to the canine as he threw the brakes on hard. This time, though it barely sufficed, the pitbull at least had a little warning that they were coming to an emergency stop. He dived back down to the seat, wrapping both front and rear legs around the cushioned leather and held on for dear life as Stone brought the huge Harley to a skidding stop, digging his heels in so hard that they dug up little furrows of dirt for about ten yards on each side of the bike.

Then he was off the Harley and running to the back, throwing open one of the biggest of the supply boxes, which he had mounted on a rack unit there. He pulled out a long silver poncho—a specially made "space blanket" Stone had dug up back in the bunker's supply room. It was supposedly impervious to caustic substances. Well, he was about to find out. Anchoring one side to the motorcycle, which was standing on its wide autokick pads on each side of the frame, Stone looked around and saw a fallen tree about a foot thick, ten feet long. He rushed behind it as Excaliber followed along curiously, his ears flapped behind him, the secondary lids on his eyes dropping down to protect him from the wind-borne sand and dust that was now flying through the air like hordes of stinging insects. Stone rolled the log back to the flapping end, and by pulling it evenly beneath the length of the tree section, he was able to anchor it solidly.

"Come on, we don't want to get caught in it," Stone yelled as he heard a sound from above and a streak of blue lightning swept across the black clouds from side to side as far he could see. He got inside the lean-to and unzipped the flaps on each side, anchoring them down with rocks. Barely had he closed them both when there was a sound like another A-bomb going off and the entire earth seemed to shake beneath them. Then there was a deluge of rain. It seemed to just release all at once, and the space blanket sagged noticeably as the first sheets of gale-blown radioactive rains came pouring down on them.

Stone pulled back closer to the Harley as if it would somehow protect him. But even the nearly one-ton vehicle rattled and bounced in the winds as if it were a bronco in a rodeo, about to be released from the starting gate. The dog whined as the thunder boomed from every side of them, and burrowned its nose into the dirt right behind Stone's leg. It covered its head and eyes with its paws and just tried to escape the horrible reality of the situation. The rain slammed into the tarp and rushed down the sides, making a little instant waterfall outside. Some of the water began seeping back underneath, and Stone lifted his body up so only his boots were touching, crouching in the darkness.

The lightning suddenly seemed to strike just outside their shelter as the entire sky lit up. For a split second Stone could see right through the material, so bright was the flash of electricity. And then, just as it faded, another, and another bolt, until the lightning was coming down in a fusillade of spears all around them. The pitbull let out a high-pitched squeal of pure fear that sent Stone's hackles up even above the deafening chorus of the storm. The booms of thunder

came galloping in one after the other, like wild horses looking to trample the shelter below, and Stone could feel his
bones shake inside his skin, as if the outer layer might just
get tossed off.

Then the rains really came. Buckets, torrents of black
water, poured down on their little haven as if it were searching them out. Liquid, as thick as sewage and as foul--
smelling as if they were in a garbage dump, inundated the
tarp, trying to get in. First a gust of dark liquid from the
east, then, unable to find an opening, the wind would switch
around to the west and spit down gushes of the filthy water,
trying to sneak in from behind them or through the spokes of
the bike, which Stone had only been partially able to cover
with part of the lower tarp flaps. Man and dog pulled in
closer and closer together, trying to get as far from the cas-
cading black foulness as they could. The dog knew in its
animal wisdom what Stone knew scientifically: that the stuff
was some bad shit.

The storm seemed to go on forever, but in reality it was
hardly five minutes, when suddenly the rains stopped almost
instantaneously, and then were gone. Stone waited a minute,
letting his heart settle down, making sure that it wasn't some
sort of trick and that one of the damn black clouds wasn't
waiting right overhead, waiting to just pour out a shitload of
the high-rad water on his head. But nothing happened, and
he nervously duck-walked over to one side and lifted the
flap. The ground around them was drenched, coated with an
oily substance that gave everything a shiny blackish tinge.
An almost invisible haze of heat fog rose up from the heat
being generated by the radioactive particles as they inter-
acted with one another from the water molecules sinking
down into the earth.

Stone looked up at the sky like a man who's just been
kicked to the ground looks up into the face of his attacker.
But the clouds had already pulled back up, high up, rejoin-
ing the miles of flat, steellike ribbons that hung in the afternoon sky, as dark and impenetrable as the black soil that
buries the dead.

Chapter Ten _____

S tone could see the effect of the rain as he drove on
toward the mountain, which now rose almost straight
up overhead. Animals writhed in pain everywhere,
their coats of fur or scales, feathers or hides, all burned and
smoking as if splashed with acid. Bald patches dotted them,
beneath which the skin was red and oozing. Many of their
eyes had been melted from the acid rains so that just an
overcooked, egglike mass dripped out of the sockets. The
radioactive rains were just taking their first dividends. Wherever they fell, Stone knew, there would be equal horror and
pain. He prayed that his men would remember to get out of
the damn rains when the clouds finally caught up with them
to the southwest.

Though he felt the urge, there was no way in hell Stone
could go out there and put all the damn suffering creatures
out of their misery. So he steeled his eyes and jaw and drove
forward, having to move slower now as the foothills were
turning to mini-mountains, and peaks loomed overhead like
skyscrapers of solid granite. But Excaliber let out little
whines of sympathy as they drove past the squealing, bel-
lowing, doomed animals, as if to let them know that someone, something, was witness to their final hour.

Within half an hour of driving on rougher and rougher
terrain, sometimes at nearly a forty-five degree angle, Stone
spotted a good cover for the Harley and brought it to a stop,
getting off and walking it the last few yards between two flat

boulders with just enough space for the bike. With a few bushes tossed over the Electraglide, no one, even if they were passing right by, would notice the motorcycle unless they stepped on the thing.

Then it was straight up the side of the mountain. Stone wasn't sure at first that the pitbull could traverse such steep, rocky slopes, but after the first few minutes, once the canine got the hang of something it had never really done before in its life, it was ahead of him the rest of the way, jumping and scrambling from one little outcropping to the next. Together, Stone doing most of the grunting, the two of them spent the rest of the afternoon climbing the mountain as the clouds lifted slightly and the sun warmed the sky to a beaten brass color.

Stone didn't have any problems at first, but as they got higher up the slope, the ground, a distant speck far below, he could feel his stomach start to turn a few somersaults. He had never been great with heights. But as there was no one to hear his excuses, after getting his breath and making a sort of mental adjustment to how high he was every few hundred feet or so, he made his way up the granite wall. The dog must have had mountain goat in its genes. For Excaliber, it was all barking and tail wagging, king of the mountain, and "What's taking you so long, asshole?" That was unquestionnably his favorite game.

As the gray sun completely disappeared behind the radioactive muck above, the world suddenly got quite dark again, and Stone reached the peak of the mountain he had been ascending. The pitbull was lying up top on its side, as if admiring the nonexistent sunset, and yawned and looked away as its struggling and sweating master dragged himself up onto the small plateau like a half-drowned sailor pulls himself onto a floating crate. It was all Stone could do to restrain himself from bopping the goddamn mutt right in the nose. But fortunately for it, he felt too exhausted to expend the energy and collapsed instead on the granite rock and lay there, panting hard, for several minutes.

At last Excaliber, actually growing worried about his motionless food supplier, rose and walked over. He licked Stone with a long, sweeping stroke of his rough, wet tongue.

Stone's eyes opened with a look of absolute fury, though he hardly moved an inch, so tired was his body.

"Get that goddamn tongue out of my face or you won't have it to fuck around with—you hear me, dog?" The pit-bull gave a final half lick with what seemed like a foot-long mop and then stepped back with a bright-eyed, busy-tailed expression and barked six times in rapid succession. If there was anything Stone hated, it was enthusiasm—especially when he could hardly move. But slowly he rose, not wanting to get caught out here when the total darkness set in. Not at the edge of a mountain with a long drop onto a floor of granite teeth.

He moved carefully across the plateau and then along a narrow ledge only about two feet wide that circled around the side of the mountain. The drop was far, to say the least, the boulders looking like little pebbles from Stone's vantage point. So he didn't look and prayed the dog wouldn't start getting too frisky. But they edged along the narrow passage for about a thousand feet in about ten minutes without any problems and reached another plateau. This one was covered with vegetation and trees and extended for nearly a mile before the next towering peak shot up like a castle tower another few thousand feet higher into the dank air.

His father, always the military man, always the special forces, the Rangers in his blood, had built the family's vacation retreat right up in the goddamn middle of nowhere, on this peak that was ten thousand feet or more up, surrounded and hidden by some of the highest mountains in the Rocky Mountain range. When the family had used the place in the past, they had driven up from the other side where the slope was much more gradual, though even then it took hours and hours of winding road to get even near the top. But Stone didn't have time for luxuries like that. It would have added a full day to his journey.

He walked along the plateau, covered with the dead undergrowth of the previous summer's vegetation. His early years up here flashed through his mind like the snapshots from a family album. How beautiful it had been in the summer, with the mountain flowers blooming golden and purple and the air always so crisp and sweet, like drinking cider from the very skies. He had enjoyed it tremendously then— a great adventure for a young boy, who would run off and disappear for hours at a time, hanging off the sides of cliffs, taking pictures of mountain goats, tangling with the bald eagles that had three families nesting around the excellently protected high cracks in the mountain's nearly vertical walls on the north and west sides. It had been a miraculous, life-filled fantasy world of color and smell. Stone had never gotten bored back then, even spending months with just his family, grandfather, and two dogs. There were no neighbors, to say the least. Just them, in the stone-hewn two-story house his father had built by hand over a period of five years. Them and the animals they shared the mountain with.

But now it was dark, cold. Everything was different. Stone knew it was bad to bring up those pictures of the past. It only brought pain. The world never would be the same again. Nor his life. There was no looking back. The ghosts were dead. The ghosts of the past had to die. Still, it hurt as he stomped silently across the ice-patched ground toward the other side. The view was spectacular, as always. As he and the dog moved quickly along the rock edges of the flat, mile-long oasis of life, they looked out over the lower Rockies off to the south where they had just come from. Even in the darkness, with just slivers of light from the full moon, like a burned-out crystal behind the curtains of radio-active cloud, he could see perhaps fifty miles. Mountain after mountain getting lower and lower as they sank in the darkness. And far, far off, the lowlands and vast patches of brown and black and gray like blurred fields from a dark dream.

It was the dog that found him first. Excaliber, as usual, had trotted on ahead to explore everything, to make sure no monsters, demons, or other dogs were waiting to attack them. But he found something else. Stone suddenly saw the pitbull about twenty yards ahead, bent down, sniffing at something.

"Good God," Stone whispered in the silvery darkness. It was a man, a naked body lying on the pebble-strewn ground atop the blanket of thick brown husks of grass. And he was mutilated horribly. A mass of wounds and holes, stabs and slices, burns and smoking holes, which Stone realized had probably been caused by the recent rains. They would have passed over here, and the guy looked like he hadn't moved for a while.

Stone kneeled down and gasped. Though it was hard even to tell, so smashed and bubbled was the face, he knew. It was Kennedy. Dr. Martin Reagan Kennedy, Snake-oil salesman extraordinaire, who had helped save his sister.

"Oh, Christ," Stone muttered, his eyes filling with tears. It wasn't fair. Why were the best the ones who always got it—instead of the slime?

"Kennedy, Doc Kennedy," Stone said, stroking at the few wisps of white hair that puffed up from the top of the bloody head. To his amazement the eyes opened, if only a slit, and two blood-filled orbs looked up at him.

"What—come back for more?" the lips hissed out almost inaudibly. "Can't you see I'm already dead, fool? But if you want to waste more time killing me, then go ahead. Go ahead." Stone could hardly believe the man was alive, let alone able to talk.

"Doc, Doc," he said, and he knelt looking down at the snakeman's battered and burn-cratered face. "It's me, Stone. Martin Stone. Remember?" The eyes somehow focused on Stone and then seemed to widen slightly. The body took in a deep breath and seemed to shiver.

"Stone—Stone, I can't believe it. How can I still be alive after what I've been through? Oh, God."

"You're cold, Doc," Stone said, charitably not mentioning the rest of Doc's condition—that he was just a corpse that had forgotten to die. The body was so terribly sliced up, still smoking from a hundred little boils that had burned right into the skin from the high-rad rains, that Stone felt a shiver rush through his own flesh as he took off his thick brown leather field jacket and laid it down over the suffering flesh.

"They've got her, Stone," Kennedy said with a forced, breathless whisper. Stone had to lean over closer to hear the man, as his lips hardly moved. "They attacked us—did this to me, took April. I heard her screaming. I—I—"

"It's okay, Doc," Stone said softly. "Save your breath. You—"

"Don't be a fool, man," Kennedy said, and his eyes caught Stone's, who saw that even inside this dying nightmare there was—for a second, anyway—the same sharp mind, the same super-aware consciousness that Stone had known when they had traveled together. "I'm dying. I know it, you know it. Let's not play." He coughed, and the frail, blood-splattered shell that was left of him, shuddered from head to toe as if in spasm. Then he relaxed again. Excaliber stood off to the side, looking curiously at the doctor. He remembered the man's smell, remembered that he had liked him, that he had given him a burning liquid that tasted wonderful and had put the dog into opium-hazed dreams for hours.

"Mafia," the thin white lips intoned so softly that Stone had to lean even farther over so that his head was only a few inches from the dying man's mouth. "Top-of-the-line pros," Kennedy went on. "Used a chopper. I heard them say, as they were dragging April off, that they were taking her to Keenesburg. They must have thought I was dead. Though— though you never know with them. Maybe they wanted me to hear. Knew you would find me."

"They can't be that good," Stone replied, his own voice sounding magnified a hundred times compared to the ghastly timbres of the dying man.

"Never underestimate them, Stone," Kennedy went on after taking a hacking, shallow breath. "Never—" Suddenly he stopped in mid-sentence and his whole face seemed to grow bright red. His back arched up so that his chest was pushed out, and it almost looked like he was trying to do a gymnastic back bend for a second or two. Which was, of course, ridiculous. He wasn't doing anything except dying. Suddenly, as if a plug had been pulled from a machine, the body completely lost all its muscular power and slammed back down onto the cold mountain ground.

Stone knew Kennedy was dead now. The body had a purplish sheen on the cheeks. He could feel the death. Feel the sudden loss of a being that had been on the side of man. That was the hardest thing for Stone—seeing the good die.

He lifted the body, keeping the jacket over the mutilated nakedness, and walked with it the few hundred yards to the stone house built right on the very edge of the mountain. The Mafia had been there, too; the place was in shambles. They had gone through everything, overturned every bureau, ripped out every closet. Looking for what? Stone couldn't imagine. It wasn't as if he or his family had hidden some secret or some object in the mountain retreat that they would have use for. No, it was just part of their modus operandi— destroy, maim, kill, and then destroy some more. They had just gotten some kicks annihilating what belonged to him and his.

Stone lay the body down on the living room table and fell back in the plush leather chair in front of the fireplace. He just sat there for a few minutes without moving, trying to control his emotions, his feelings of absolute deadness. Excaliber came up alongside and, feeling exhausted now itself, sat down beside the chair and put its head in its paws, shivering its fur up and down, trying to create some warmth, as it was freezing in the unheated stone house, the mountain winds outside blowing through myriad cracks in the place as the night set in.

Stone rose at last, threw some logs into the fireplace, and after a few minutes got a decent blaze going. But there was one more thing he had to do before he could rest. He walked to the corpse of Dr. Kennedy, took his jacket off it, and looked down at the frail old man. He hadn't been that big to begin with, and after what the bastards had done to him, and then the rains . . . Stone knew he couldn't let the corpse stay here overnight. There were wolves in these mountains. They would smell it quickly and would attack the stone shelter, which, without windows, courtesy of the Mafia hit men, would allow them entry. He walked to one of the bedrooms and ripped a sheet from a bed, then wrapped the corpse in the long cotton sheet until it was bound tightly like a mummy. He went to the kitchen and found a can of kerosene.

"Stay here, dog," Stone said as he lifted the package of death over his shoulder. "What I'm going to do—I don't want you to see. Remember him in health and life, okay?" The animal turned from its place on the rug in front of the fire, as if Stone must be mad even to think that the animal would consider such a suggestion. Then it turned forward again to soak up as many of the hot, crackling rays as it could before cruel reality intruded again.

Stone carried the load outside and to the edge of the mountain that the house was built on, only about ten yards off. It was as if they were in the clouds, up there with the gods, higher than any of the slopes ahead, just darkness and curtains of mist swallowing up the land below. He lay the body down and sprinkled it with the kerosene until almost every square inch of the sheet was damp. In the sky above, the aurora borealis suddenly appeared as if a mirage, a vision. The ghostly drifting patterns of red and blue and yellow and green wove down subtle hues of twisted color across the dead man's face.

"A funeral for a brave man," Stone said as he flicked his Ronson all-weather lighter. "The kind the Vikings and the Indians used to give for their noblest warriors." He leaned down and touched the tongue of blue to the sheet, and it burst instantly into flame. Within seconds the pyre was roaring, and there was just a solid wall of fire in front of him. He waited a few seconds to let the fire reach inside, too, until everything was burning, everything being purified by the flames, every bit of the filth and dirt of life being washed off for the journey to wherever.

" 'Bye, pal," Stone said softly, and he kicked forward with his foot so the burning sheet sailed suddenly over the edge into black space. It seemed to burn like a meteor, lighting up the mountain walls around with its sudden, incandescent glow. Then the sheet unraveled, and the burning body spun wildly in the night air below, arms and legs all spiraling out in a crazy dance as tongues of white fire licked over every part of the falling man. And Stone watched the legs and arms became a solid shape and then just a dot of yellow. And at last, as far as he could see below, into the valleys of gray fog, there was nothing. The old man had been eaten by the predator night.

Chapter Eleven _____

When Stone awoke the next morning, he was lying in the leather chair in front of the burned down fire with his Uzi in his right hand and his Ruger .44 lying on the armrest of the chair next to his left. Maybe he was getting just a little paranoid, Stone thought to himself as he sat there for a few seconds without moving an inch. But paranoia was the philosophy of those who survived.

He looked into the glowing embers and saw the ghosts dancing there again, bloody, ephemeral mists that seemed to play tag among the stark blue fingers of flame.

"Oh, Christ." Stone groaned out loud. There was something about waking up knowing that all you were going to face that day were murderers, cannibals, wolves, God knew what all. . . . That made a man just want to close his lids and dive into the gray beyond for a few more hours. But he knew he couldn't. April was out there, and he didn't want to think about what might be happening to her.

"Fucking foot," he sputtered as he tried to rise from the chair but discovered that his foot had fallen asleep from the slightly peculiar position he had been sleeping in. He heard a similar snort of expletives from his side and looked down to see the pitbull stretched out on his back, basking in the last few strokes of warmth from the fading fire. The pitbull didn't look like he wanted to go outside into the damp, radioactive cold, either.

"We've gotta split, dog," Stone said, rising at last as he

looked down at the animal. One thing about the dog—it knew how to suck in every goddamn ounce of pleasure it could find. He hobbled on his still half-numb foot into the kitchen where he was happy to discover that the hit men who had wrecked the place had at least left the Maxwell House. Within minutes he and the dog were sipping deep drafts of black brew from his dead mother's best china.

Outside, it was just about as wretched as Stone had imagined. The sky was as dark as ever, though the high, thick cloud cover seemed to have broken up into long strips, almost rings of different colors. A black ring, then a brownish color, then an almost greenish one—each area of color perhaps ten, fifteen miles wide. Something was going on up there, but he sure as hell didn't want to know about it. Even in the dim morning he could see for miles and miles to the west and south—where he would be heading—mountainous, jagged hills and dense pockets of forest. Much farther on, he saw another higher range of mountains—perhaps seventy-five miles off. He wished he'd eaten his fucking Wheaties, not that there were any to be had for blood or money.

The bullterrier jumped up onto the back of the black Harley before Stone had even reached it, and clamped itself around the seat as if it were in love with it. Stone plopped down on the front portion and turned the "instant start." It roared up in less than a second, and shifting into gear, he started slowly ahead down the steep road. In the freezing morning air, the condensed dew along the road had turned to ice and formed little puddles of sheer slickness. Stone had to slow to about five miles per hour, moving along with both his feet out on each side, sliding along the ground as if he were skiing. He didn't want to go over up here.

This worked fine until he had gone about two hundred yards down the winding mountain road, which was hardly wider than a bathtub. But then both his feet and the front wheel of the bike hit a large frozen patch at the same instant. Before he knew it, everything was going sideways, and Stone found himself sliding along the icy sheen with the bike on top of him. He heard barking, and his ear scraped along the road so that it sounded like a bomb was going off. Suddenly everything came to a stop, and there was total silence. Stone tried to move, but he was virtually pinned down by the weight of the Harley, though as far as he could tell, nothing had been broken. He managed to tilt his head around at a forty-five-degree angle and gulped hard when he saw what lay there.

He was lying at the very edge of a granite abyss that dropped down at least three thousand feet before reaching spears of rock like punji sticks implanted by nature. His head and shoulder were just over the edge, the rest of him was trapped under the bike, which Stone suddenly saw, to his horror, was also partially hanging over the side. The weight balance between staying up and going down was not particularly great. He could see that in a sickening glance.

Stone pulled his head back, as he didn't particularly want to look down at the great drop. It made his heart beat like a drum machine on speed. He tried not to panic, not letting his body move a muscle. What would his father have done? Stone suddenly found himself thinking. What would Major Clayton R. Stone, ex-superfighter, have done? It seemed, Stone realized suddenly, that he always wondered what the old man would have done when he got himself into tight situations. But what the hell. The son of a bitch knew his stuff—even if the two of them hadn't seen eye to eye. But his father had been dead for months now, while he, on the other hand, was here, stuck between nearly a ton of cold metal, perched on the end of a mountain, like Humpty Dumpty on the wall. And Stone knew that if he fell off *this* wall, nothing would put his ass together again.

Suddenly he felt a shifting weight above him, as if something were running over the top, and then Excaliber appeared, peering down from the steel-alloy body of the Harley, dropping his paws over the edge, with a big tongue-hanging smile on his white-and-brown face. He stared down at Stone curiously, wagging his tail, begging with wide eyes to be let in on the game.

"Dog, you'd better get your fucking ass off this bike," Stone screamed out in a mad bellow. The pitbull was so startled by the explosion of sound that it nearly threw itself backward and onto the ground. The whole bike wobbled back and forth above Stone, as if debating whether to topple over now or wait a few minutes so Martin Stone's brain could be messed with a little more. It apparently decided on the latter course of action, for the 1200-cc bike suddenly dropped back over onto the dirt with a thud and settled down again.

Stone let his pounding heart slow down to about half its chest-bursting gallop and took a deep breath.

"Excaliber," he yelled, though the sound didn't come out with a great amount of projection, as his chest was pinned by part of the seat and he could only inhale about a third of his regular lung power. "Excaliber," Stone wheezed out again. This time he heard an answering bark from the other side of the bike.

"Pull bike," Stone said commandingly. "Pull the bike! Bike, bike! Pull the fucking bike, you hear me!" He realized he was getting louder with each word and that his whole body was shaking. The bike started acting up above him, and Stone shut up again, making himself relax and calm down. He was in no great shakes to hasten his great ski jump into the beyond. The pitbull barked again, seemed to think about the words, and then Stone heard what could only be described as stone scraping along metal. He felt the bike shudder above him and realized that the animal had bitten into some part of it. And indeed, hidden from view on the other side, the canine had sunk his incisors into part of the long tailpipe that ran down the lower right back portion of the Harley. With the greatest pound-per-square-inch bite in the dog kingdom, the pitbull actually managed to snap right through the metal so that the tips of the its teeth were inside the piping.

Setting itself, the animal began pulling with all it had. But nothing seemed to happen. As Stone felt the angle of the bike shift just an inch or so and then stop, he realized that part of the bike must be digging into the ground, hitting it at an angle and stopping it from moving any farther. Stone tried to shake his foot to get the animal's attention. He sent out the command to shake, anyway, but his legs—all squeezed up beneath the Harley—just sort of vibrated weakly.

"Grab my pants, dog," Stone screamed out again. "The pants, the pants!" With all he had, he exerted himself to wiggle the foot around and then collapsed again as the movement put a tremendous strain on the tendons and muscles of his leg. The pitbull let go of the exhaust pipe and approached the oddly moving foot, sniffing hard at it four times. It looked up at the bike, back down at the foot, and then seemed to put two and two together. The dog carefully lowered itself down to ground level and, opening its jaws, moved them forward over the pants leg as carefully as a mother handling her pups, making sure not to bite Stone or even break the skin. When it had its jaws up over the pants about three inches or so, the dog clamped down hard, and its teeth bit through the thick denim like a bear trap.

Excaliber set himself so that his whole body was aiming backward, while his legs bent forward at about a forty-five degree angle. Then he pulled. At first nothing seemed to happen at all, beyond the strong denim material stretching out an inch or two and the dog straining. When the material had been stretched to its absolute fullest and the dog saw that it hadn't torn, he seemed to switch into second gear. Letting out a high-pitched squeal from between his closed jaws, the pitbull leaned back even more sharply, so that he was pulling the load at an almost horizontal angle.

Stone felt like his leg was about to be ripped off, but he bit his lip and shut up. He knew this was his only chance. The dog pulled and pulled, expending incredible energy. Every muscle in its body seemed to stand out like ropes across its rippling, shiny pelt. And suddenly the bike moved. Not a lot at first, just a half inch, but for the first time since he'd looked down, Stone started to think that perhaps he'd actually come out of all this in one piece. With the heavy denim fabric and Stone's leg, almost acting like a slide beneath it, the big Harley started shifting forward inch by grudging inch.

The pitbull pulled until the machine came forward about a foot, and then stopped, stepped back with all fours, setting itself again in a perfect angle against the machine to give himself the greatest leverage. If a super-computer had calculated the exact angle to pull the bike at for maximum effect, it would have come to the same figure that the canine did by instinct. After about a dozen such pulls, Stone yelled for the dog to stop again. He looked down and saw that he was off the edge, looking down at gravel and dead patches of grass. Now free of danger, he was able to struggle and slide around with all his strength—and within a minute or so managed to extricate himself from the death trap.

"Good fucking dog," Stone said as he stood up and walked around the back of the bike where the animal sat, looking all puffed up about his feat of strength. "Yeah, I know, I'll make sure you get a medal from the President." He scratched the pitbull between the ears, and it let out a little yawn of bored narcissism. "Come on, let's get the hell out of here—before something else happens." Stone righted the Harley with some effort. On its side, it was like a few thousand pounds of turtle that had tumbled onto its back. But then it was up—and it seemed undamaged. The whole side was scraped free of paint, but it was used to a lot worse than that.

They remounted, and Stone went extra slow down the road, this time his hands squeezing the brakes with constant little motions. It took them hours to get all the way to the bottom and back onto a flat and iceless two-laner that headed straight west. Like all the roads and highways of America, this one had cracks and grass sprouting through myriad little holes and slits in it. But it was traversable, and Stone let the bike edge up in speed, hitting first thirty, then forty, until he was cruising along in the dim twilight of the early afternoon at fifty-plus. The dog was fully alert today, having finally had even a dog's fill of sleep it had caught in front of the fire the night before. It rested its front paws up on each side of Stone's leather-jacketed back and wrapped its back legs forward and around the sides of the leather seat so that it appeared to be riding the thing sitting upright, which it was. The pitbull's head scanned back and forth to each side of the road, fascinated by the speeding terrain. Its eyes moved like little slot-machine fruits as it tried to catch and focus on any particular object, which was impossible. But that didn't stop the pitbull from trying until it was as dizzy as a spinning child and started feeling its morning coffee threatening to rise up from its usually cast-rion stomach.

Stone kept a sharp eye on the speeding landscape as they moved along. He knew that the hunters of the world struck when you didn't see them—not when you did. His eye took in every tree ahead, every boulder that loomed toward them, every rise, every patch of thick pine forest. Took them in, searched them, scanned them for a glint of steel, the motion of a bush, for anything abnormal. For Stone was a predator too. And he knew how to hunt the hunters. But other than eyes here and there, and the rustle of leaves off on the sides of the road, there was nothing.

After about an hour Stone began running into wrecks of cars. He passed just a few at first, their rusting hulks oddly serene in the midst of the weed-sprinkled two-laner. The glass on them and all removable parts had long since vanished, but the basic frames remained, slowly rotting, sinking lower toward the roadway, until they became the roadway, nothing but a brownish-red coating of oxidized steel. Eventually they would melt into the roadway itself, would sink into the earth and— Stone made himself stop musing on such metaphysical postulations on the ultimate decay of the entire universe, though riding along these roads filled with steel corpses, it was hard to avoid.

The cars became more frequent as Stone approached an ancient intersection where several Interstates came together at once. The great, curving ramps of concrete that had once supported millions of cars yearly were now just broken-down and collapsed ruins. Like the Roman monuments that had once seemed the glory of the world, eternal, unsmash-able, so America's great highways were now finding their destiny in dust. Stone had to laugh. It was all rubble. Not even passable anymore by car. Only a motorcycle could drive through the debris. He slowed to a stop as they came underneath an overpass that was still in one piece, though the roadway at each end had come free of the actual moor-ings, so it just sort of stood there on rows of cement pillars like an aqueduct going nowhere.

"Let them try to figure that one out." Stone smirked at the

dog as he stepped off the bike. "Future aliens from space studying civilization here on earth. When they try to decipher what this single bridge in the middle of nowhere is—" Stone laughed. The pitbull jumped down and looked up, trying to understand the intellectual heights to which its master was attempting to lead it.

Stone walked around in a little circle, trying to undo the cramps that had begun setting in along his right leg. He had been shot, wounded, slammed, he'd taken every goddamn thing you could do to the human body. It was a wonder he could walk at all. But this particular spasming pain along his calf had become intolerable. He sat down on a barn-door-size chunk of roadway that lay buried sideways in the dirt and massaged the leg with his hands, trying to work the pain free.

Out of the corner of his eye Stone saw the pitbull run off about thirty yards to a whole bunch of the wrecked vehicles, all lying piled among one another, as if it were a burial ground for dead automobiles. Stone glanced up to gauge the intentions of the dead-man's sky and didn't like what he saw. Some of the darker, ringlike radioactive clouds were starting to swoop down again, as if heading toward the earth, to strangle it in their poison rains.

He lowered his head to whistle for the pitbull, and his eyes opened wide. As the animal played atop the roof of a rusting van, so that its leg broke through here and there as it pranced about, Stone saw something it didn't. A brown blanket of moving creatures coming out of the other wrecks that surrounded it. Tens of thousands of them, hundreds of thousands, sweeping out of their filthy, rusted metal lairs with a rapid motion, brown feelers rippling madly as they searched out the enemy that had intruded in their ranks.

"Dog!" Stone screamed at the top of his lungs, cupping both hands around his mouth. "Look out, look down, down!" Stone pointed with both hands toward the approaching armies of brown horror as he started hobbling back toward the bike, a few yards behind him. The dog followed his motion, and as its head went down, its own eyes opened in abject terror. The animal was not afraid of another living animal on this earth, but bugs—especially cockroaches—

were another story. It let out an ear-shattering, high-pitched
squeal of terror, baying up into the air for a second. Then it
looked down again and saw that it was completely cut off.
The things were coming from everywhere, the ground for a
good twenty feet in all directions just a moving ocean of
brown and black roaches. All coming straight toward him.

Stone reached the Harley and started it up. Again he
cupped his hands and yelled out to the canine. "Jump, you
son of a bitch. Jump, you hear me?" He pointed from the
dog to the bike a few times and then started the engine,
revving it hard. He knew it was mean—for now the animal
was afraid he was going to leave it, and that it was about to
be eaten wholesale by an army of radiation's most beloved
little pets.

But it worked. For as Stone slowly let out the clutch and
started the 1200-cc forward, the pitbull took one final look
as the front ranks of the roaches reached the very edge of the
brown Caddy roof he was standing on. Flexing his muscular
legs down like little steel pistons, the bullterrier suddenly
launched himself forward from the side. It was like a furry
rocket had taken off, as the combined strength of the animal's innate power, mixed with its adrenaline at the approaching roach army, with a dash of pure hate at Stone for
daring to leave it, all combined to propel it forward. Stone
watched in amazement as the animal curled itself up into a
ball so that it actually seemed to catch wind at a right angle
to keep it going.

At last, after a flight of perhaps twenty-five feet, just
enough to land it in the very outer reaches of the wriggling
brown bodies, the dog came down hard into a small group of
them, squashing dozens beneath its paws. Letting out a yelp
of disgust, the bullterrier shot forward, darting over the rows
of roaches like a hundred yard dash prospect for the Olym-
pics. Stone started the bike forward, coming up at an angle
so that he would intersect the dog just past the blanket of
brown. As he came by at about fifteen miles per hours, Ex-
calibur, at a full run, jumped again and came down like a
swan with both wings cut off into the backseat, sliding forward and slamming into Stone so that he almost dislodged
him.

Stone somehow managed to keep the Electraglide upright, motivated by the desire not to end up as cockroach soufflé on this beautiful radioactive evening. With both of them bouncing around like two psychotic men in a tub, the Harley shot forward over the rough broken pieces of roadway beneath the overpass. Stone did all he could to keep the bike going, as they shot back and forth between the oddly angled slabs like billiard balls. At last he came down hard on solid road, and they were suddenly upright and on basically level ground. Stone floored the Harley without even looking back, shooting along the two-laner that headed due west straight into the darkest part of the radioactive cloud cover, the burial blanket for mankind.

The advance scouts of the cockroach army reached the roof of the rusted Caddy, and their four flanks joined feelers, coming up from every part of the car. Their waving tendrils patted along the nearly powdered crystal surface of the rusted metal and up into the air, as if their quarry were somehow hanging there like a balloon. But however he had done it, he was gone. A fair-sized dinner disappeared just when it was within mandibles' reach. After scurrying around the car for nearly twenty minutes, as the information that the dog had disappeared was conveyed to all, the insects began retreating back into their filth-coated homes inside the decayed hulks, in ravenous and pissed-off moods.

Chapter Twelve

Stone didn't even pause to take a breath until they'd gone ten miles. The thought of the blanket of little squirming brown creatures did something to the center of his guts. Like his dog, Stone had problems with the idea of being eaten alive by insects too. But apparently that had just been a pocket of them, as they weren't swarming out from every tree. Still, Stone realized he'd been seeing more and more of the little bastards since the bomb had gone off. The radiation either forced them from their burrows—or perhaps they were attracted by the multitude of dead things to eat. Carnivorous cockroaches. It made him shudder. In a few more years, if things kept going the way they were, there would doubtless be only roaches, sharks, and rats left on the damn planet, anyway. And they'd look around one day and realize that all their victims were gone. And they'd turn and stare at one another—and then go at it tooth and nail, until there was nothing left on the planet. Not a single living, breathing thing.

"There I go again," Stone said, berating himself as he eased back in the seat a little. "I must have the most fatalistic brain this side of the torture chambers." But when he thought about it, the sheer fact that he was alive and not in the gizzards of an entire suburb of roaches was something to cheer about. They drove on what was fairly flat land for about twenty miles, and Stone made good time. Then the two-laner turned to an asphalt one-laner that seemed to have been in the wrenching hands of an earthquake or something. As he rode along it, the road got so bad that, in disgust, Stone at last just rode right off the road and through the meadows and meandering hills.

But by twilight the sloping rises had turned to foothills, and the going got rougher and rougher, the trees in thicker bunches so that he kept having to skirt dense sections, zig-zagging all over the damn Rockies. He tried to push it as night fell fast but found it almost impossible to keep going, so rough was the terrain; so dim was the light that soon they were moving just a few miles per hour, bouncing up and down like yo-yos as the bike's tires went over ditches, bumps, every damn thing that mottled the flesh of the hills.

At last, exasperated and wanting to keep going but know-ing, after his experience that morning, how easy it was to die if you didn't watch your ass, Stone came to a stop as he spotted a bunch of boulders side by side at the foot of a thousand-foot slope off to the left. He pulled the Harley right up to the edge of one of the high boulders and, taking a few supplies along, hauled himself up the ten feet or so to the top, where a fairly flat space about six feet in diameter would make passable sleeping quarters. The dog made sev-eral running jumps, and then, using the seat of the Harley as a launching pad, it managed to jump up so that its front paws just made the top, and with some frantic clawing against the rock below it with its back paws, the dog at last pulled itself up and quickly turned to survey the area below and around them. The first thing it ever did was check out the defensive and offensive capabilities of any situation. It was bred into the animal's genes to think, live, breathe, and dream of battle. Of tigers, and men with knives, of unknown nightmares, creatures that lived in its unconscious, its deep-est, darkest fears.

And it swore it saw some of them skulking around off in the shadows of the trees that spread off around them. The pitbull whined and looked up at Stone, who was kneeling, spreading out a bedroll along the rock.

"Oh, don't be such a fucking coward," Stone admonished the animal as it sighted—or thought it did—something in a thicket of bush about thirty yards off. At last the pitbull

settled down, folding its legs under it and bringing its head
to rest on its front paws. It appeared to be asleep. But that's
only what it wanted any attackers in the dark to believe.
Actually it always had at least one eye opened just a slit,
surveying the entire area. Stone found the most comfortable
position he could muster up on a piece of quarter-inch-thick
blanket atop a granite boulder sheared smooth by Ice Age
glaciers. Which wasn't very comfortable. He knew the dog
would keep an eye on things. Sometimes the animal's general anxiety was very useful, at least to Stone, for knowing
that the slightest crack of a twig in the woods would have
the animal up and ready to go airborne, Stone actually became relaxed enough to fall into a quick and deep sleep.

When he awoke, it was almost pitch-black out, but for
the eerie glow of the aurora forcing its light through the high
clouds. He sat up and saw Excaliber standing by the edge of
the boulder. His nose and tail were lined up as he stood, set
in his pointing—and hunting—stance. Stone followed the
line of canine fire and saw eyes, three pairs of them—red
and burning in the darkness, almost as if from their own
light. He could dimly make out large, dark, furred shapes
just at the line of trees. They looked larger than wolves, but
Stone couldn't see clearly. The pitbull was emitting an almost subsonic growl that Stone just heard the edge of. But
he knew the night eaters out there heard it. For similar low
but equally threatening sounds emerged.

Stone knew they saw him now, and he loosened his Uzi,
which he had worn in his sleep, around his chest in its holster. Apparently that was too much, for the red eyes seemed
to blaze brightly for a moment like a spark fanned with
wind, and then they were gone, just like that, and where
they had stood were just pockets of darkness and the occasional call from a nervous bird. Stone lay himself back down
as the pitbull continued to hold its stance. This time it took
him almost an hour to fall asleep again. And his dreams
were bad.

When he awoke again, he could see that it was morning.
Or what would have to pass as morning, anyway. The light
dribbled down in gray puddles through the black clouds that
rolled by, miles up. Stone knew the sun must have been

positively burning down through the upper atmosphere, bright as a searchlight, for more light was actually reaching him this morning than he'd seen for days. Still, he found himself yearning for real sun, blue sky. The things one took for granted seemed suddenly priceless when they were snatched away. The constant darkness was getting to him. Making him feel more like a corpse than a man. Living in the darkness and semidarkness like bugs and spiders hidden beneath logs and deep in caves.

Stone and the pitbull scrambled down the side of the boulder and quickly mounted the Harley. There wasn't a trace of their night visitors, though Stone kept his holster's flap open and the safety off on his Uzi autopistol. At least he could see in the gray mist and was able to get the bike up to about twenty miles per hour; it was still a bumpy journey as they bounced through the foothills. Then they were back on some kind of road that cut up into the higher mountain ahead, on the other side of which Stone calculated the road should bring him to within a few miles of Keenesburg. It better.

Stone positively floored the Electraglide once he saw that the road wasn't in terrible shape. It was funny how some of them went like rotten fruit and others seemed unscathed, ready to stand up for another hundred years. Probably all depended on who was getting paid off when they had been built—and how inferior the quality of Mafia concrete had been, Stone thought cynically.

He reached the peak of the final mountain around three in the afternoon and could see down for miles onto the far side. He took out his field binocs and tried to find the town, or whatever it was. There—perhaps ten miles off to the west —was some sort of habitation. Though all he could see was the cluster of buildings, nothing in greater detail than yards wide. Stone put the field glasses away and, checking around to make sure that the damn dog wasn't off chasing a venomous snake or grizzly bear or some damn thing, took off down the descending road.

They had gone perhaps two miles when Stone, just rounding a curve, had to slam on the brakes to avoid crashing into a man walking along the road. He was as naked as the day he was born and covered with wounds and sores dripping a thick pus from numerous red openings. Stone could see they were radiation burns, for the man's arms and back were covered with the raised red welts that were literally melting off him—like Leaping Elk's blob of a hand before he had been sent to hell. But this one didn't seem dangerous, just out of it. *Zombie* might be a better word for it, for as Stone came alongside the slowly walking figure, he could see that the man's eyes were gone as old marbles, dead and dull. He was just somehow clomping one foot down, then the other, mumbling something to himself as he walked.

"Hey, pal," Stone yelled out, but the man didn't budge an inch or even deign to glance over at his caller. "Suit yourself," Stone said, and started forward again. He wasn't about to stop and get into an encounter therapy session with the naked, pus-ridden fellow to find out why the poor lad was so shy. Not today.

But he had scarcely gone a hundred yards when Stone saw it was going to have to be group therapy if he was going to open a practice for the insane soon-to-be-dead. For there was another one and, in front of him, another. In fact, there was a whole line of them straggling along with all the enthusiasm of those about to attend the Inquisition. And all naked and covered with the same dripping red sores and welts, their skin nothing but bubbles and foam in many places. The hair on all of them had all fallen out, and they were as bald as eggs, though these were bloody eggs, as the skin atop the skulls had started rotting to the consistency of week-old pumpkin.

Stone slowed down, keeping both feet on the ground and his fingers on the trigger of the Harley's 50-cal. mounted up front. But these dudes weren't dangerous. Except to his stomach. As he watched, they beat at their already decimated frames. They whipped at themselves with belts and branches filled with thorns, pounded at their shoulders and their heads with rocks until their hands were red. Even the pitbull stared at the scene with revolted fascination. And as they stumbled along like the army of the walking dead,

Stone could hear them half whispering, almost singing to themselves:

> "You are poison, you are rot,
> You must die, must be not,
> You are filth, you are scum,
> Smash your flesh, make you brains run."

And other such cheerful verses, at least as far as Stone could make out, though it was hard to really tell, as they mumbled in a singsong way through toothless, lipless, and, in some cases, tongueless mouths. It made for quite a chorus as he wheeled slowly down the road, passing dozens of them, each one in a worse state of decay and imminent danger of popping than the one before him. At last he reached what appeared to be the very front of the line, as he could see down the yellow-lined road ahead for nearly a mile and there wasn't another figure. He pulled up alongside the "leader." He, too, was naked and covered with the pus-oozing blisters and boils, the whole chunks of skin falling from his body. It was like looking at something in a state of constant decomposition, every step making a piece jar loose, something pop and spit out a gush of red and brown. This one at least was doing something besides falling apart. He was swinging an ancient family-sized tin can that had once been filled with pickles back and forth in front of him. Only now it was burning a fatty subtance like melted wax but with a distinctly sour and sickening smell. The man sputtered as he walked, sending out a spray of spittle in front of him like a fine mist with every word:

> "I must rot, I must fall,
> I must bleed and scream and crawl . . ."

"Uh, howdy, stranger," Stone said as he pulled the bike up alongside the lead scout of the naked stumblers. "Nice day, huh?" This one at least acknowledged him, Stone saw as the man turned his head slightly toward the intruder, without breaking stride, without letting the lamp that emitted a little chimney of thick gray smoke from stopping its pendulum swing back and forth as if driving the demons off ahead by choking them. The man's eyes caught Stone's, and he felt a shudder rush up and down his body like a snake undulating down a log. For the man only had what looked like the beginnings of a face. The muscles were there in plain sight, many of the veins lying there like red-and-blue strings wriggling slightly like so many worms as they continued to pump their diseased radioactive blood through the rotting physique. It was as if the face hadn't been finished, had never had the skin put on it, the features drawn in. Just two wet, dark balls, like olives in a martini of blood and slime, peered back at him from within what had been a man's face.

"If you don't mind my being a little nosy?" Stone said with as cheerful a grin as he could muster under the circumstances. "Just why are you fellows—uh—taking a walk naked, and, you know, hitting yourselves and all that?"

"We must be punished," the man croaked back, and Stone tried to keep the smile on his face as the little tubes of red flesh that were the man's lips wriggled up and down, the two teeth that were left in the oozing mouth, hanging by threads, swinging back and forth as he spoke, as if they might tumble out at any moment. "We are God's chosen. Chosen to die for man's sins." The man groaned and suddenly reached up with his free hand and smashed himself in the head with a hammer.

Stone involuntarily winced, as did the pitbull behind him, and he was starting to get edgy about the sick scene unfolding in front of them. When Stone opened his eyes a split second later, the man was reeling from the blow, a hole the size of a quarter opened right in the side of his skull as a pinkish, gruellike substance flowed out like Silly Putty. Yet still the man kept walking, lurching forward on legs that were hardly more than gangrenous stalks held together by sheer pressure onto the cracking, rubbery bones beneath them.

"Why—must you be punished?" Stone went on, wanting to just floor the bike ahead but somehow needing to know the reason for the group's bizarre behavior.

"Man has sinned. That is why he is being destroyed. By punishing ourselves we are helping God. Carrying out his work." The man smiled a red hole of a smile, as if pleased with his explanation. "All must die. But we are hastening the process. And causing ourselves great pain. As much pain as possible. That is the whole idea. That is the punishment. Blessed be the self-mutilators, for they are carrying out the atomic judgment's work." Again he smiled, and the red hole opened and closed again like the jaws of some wretched creature from a nightmare.

"I s-see," Stone stuttered, unable to argue with such logic. "Well, well—good luck," he muttered, realizing as the words left his lips how absurd they were. But the man either didn't hear them or was unable to relate to the inherent absurdity of the statement. Instead he whipped the hammer up again at his head, and it sank nearly an inch into and through the rotting skull. He seemed to stagger again, sinking down almost to his knees. But then somehow, incredibly, the mobile piece of rot regained his balance and kept on. And as Martin Stone swore that what he was seeing was just about the most horrible thing he'd ever encountered, he saw something worse. For the walking ooze, noticing through cracked, bleeding eyes that the little fire in its pot was burning low, reached toward itself with a scooping hand, its fingers all stiff, and dug the hand right into its side, where Stone could see it had previously scooped out a bunch.

It poked around into its own innards as it walked, hardly faltering and, after a few seconds of digging, ripped out a whole big batch of human rot. It swung the hand around and threw the load on top of the low blue flames as the last of the old fire almost went out. There was a sudden sheet of blue and yellow as the radioactive slime caught fire in a flash. A cloud of yellowish smoke rose up all around them, making Stone and the dog cough and wave it away from their faces.

"Jesus fucking Christ," Stone half screamed as he floored the bike forward, trying to get out of the nauseating mist. He exhaled hard as he shot away from the line of moaning men, who continued to slice and beat at themselves with great enthusiasm. He breathed deeply in and out, trying to get the filthy poison out of his lungs. The dog, too, seemed to hyperventilate, whether through instinct or realizing that the human smoke was bad, Stone didn't know. But the two of them, man and animal, took deep filling breaths of air, pushing out from the very bottom of their lungs for the next twenty minutes as they rode along. Stone didn't know if the stuff could really hurt him or not. But it sure hadn't done the fellow from whom it had come any good.

Chapter Thirteen _____

By the time they reached the outskirts of Keenesburg, Stone still didn't feel like he had really laundered his lungs. He felt dirty and wanted nothing more than to find a bath, try to clean the stench of decay and rot off him. The dog kept snorting and sneezing and scratching at itself, as if it were covered with fleas. Stone found a small garage/stable at the very outer perimeter of the town, a ramshackle place that no one else apparently was using, since neither a vehicle nor a single horse or mule sat in the broken-down, fenced-in area, or in the half-collapsed barn, framed on each side by trees.

The place was out-of-the-way, almost nonexistent—the kind of place Stone loved. He came to a stop just in front of a little shack—hardly more than a bunch of warped pieces of plywood nailed up into a square about six feet high and eight feet long. It was hard to believe someone would live in it, but from the little trickle of smoke rising up out of the chimney made from an old paint can on top, Stone had to assume that was the case. And sure enough, when he dismounted and knocked on what he deducted was the door as all four sides looked pretty much the same, an old man, as ancient-looking as the face of the desert, pushed out on the wall so that it swung around on crude hinges, and stepped out. He carried a shotgun in his arms and tried to look as mean as possible, though standing about 4'10" and being hardly more than a shriveled-up raisin of an old man with a thousand lines creasing his leathery face, fingers as thin as pencils, he wasn't too fear-inspiring.

"What the hell you want?" the old man asked suspiciously, squinting one bloodshot eye at Stone.

"Sorry if I'm in the wrong place," Stone said, holding his hand slowly up in the air to show he meant no harm. "I thought I saw a sign out there by the road that said 'garage.'"

The old man laughed a short and bitter sound and then said. "No, ain't been no garage here for years. Ain't been no fuel, no nothing. And since my son died—the bastards killed him"—the man went on looking toward the town in the distance and spitting at it—"ain't done much of nothing but sit around and wait to die." The old codger, whom Stone estimated had to be at least ninety-five or a hundred years old gave him a big grin, his mouth filled with wooden teeth, as if the statement were quite amusing.

"Well, look, if you're just sitting around waiting to die," Stone said, moving his hand slowly into his pocket so as not to startle the man, "why not make a few bucks doing it?" He took out two silver dollars from a stack he had filled a pocket with, coins he'd taken from his father's bunker supplies. Stone had learned quickly after leaving the bunker, having lived there for five years, that money was worth a hell of a lot more than it had been before. And that a silver dollar was enough for men to kill for.

The man's eyes grew wide at the proffered coins, shining in the few straggly rays of gray light that sputtered down from the fallout sheets ten miles up, just sitting up there looking down on them all like the cloaked judges of doom.

"Name's Lomax," the man said, suddenly as friendly as a summer day. "But people around here always called me Pliers, on account I always been good with my hands." He took the coins from Stone's palm and drew them to him like the most precious things in the world. He held them up, turning them over in his hand, almost hypnotized by the clear shininess of their perfect surfaces.

"What I gotta do?" he asked, suddenly suspicious again, and the grin of incredible luck vanished from his face like it had never existed. The possibility that he would suddenly lose the little beauties that he regarded with an almost religious awe made a ratlike paranoia streak into his brain like mercury rising in a thermometer.

"Just let me park my motorcycle in that barn," Stone said, turning and pointing to his Harley, about twenty yards off. At the back part of the black leather seat, Excaliber was trying to find a comfortable position as he twisted this way and that on the cool leather, wriggling his paws in the air as if performing some insane dance. "And take care of that there dog too." Stone prayed that the old fellow liked dogs, because too many people were after him, and those people would know about the dog as well. It would stand out in the town like a sore thumb. Not that Stone had any illusions that he wasn't walking into a trap, anyway. But he wasn't one to place the fucking noose over his head and pull the trapdoor as well.

"Bike and dog—that's all, mister?" the old man said with a laugh of relief as he saw that he was going to get to keep his little fortune, after all. "Why, I loves dogs. In fact . . ." He whistled twice, and a scampering sound came from inside the plywood hut. Before Stone could warn him to stop, a dog came tearing out and straight toward the bike. It was the strangest damn little thing Stone had ever seen—a hybrid of hybrids, a mixture of every breed under the sun—only about twenty pounds of furry little dachshundy thing, with, Stone saw in growing amazement, only three legs. The fourth had been chopped off about two thirds of the way up, so the dog scampered along on three but, all things considered, with speed and balance.

"Excaliber!" Stone screamed out, raising his arm as the pitbull saw the little barking fuzzball coming toward the bike. Stone knew the animal had never gotten along with other dogs—it wasn't in his blood. The pitbull rose up in a flash onto the seat and launched itself free with a powerful stroke of pistonlike legs. Stone groaned and closed his eyes for a second, unable to witness the chomping, bloody mess that was about to occur. But when Stone opened his eyes, there was no blood at all. Instead the two dogs stood almost face-to-face, though Excaliber had to look down, as the small mutt was hardly bigger than a cat. Still, the thing gave one of the canine terrors of Colorado a firm but friendly look, and the bullterrier, being impressed by the sheer tenacity of the little sucker, took an instant liking to him and began playing lightly with the dog, running this way and that in front of it, suddenly changing direction as the overfurred mutt joined in the fun.

"Well, looks like those two hit it off," Stone said with a look of disbelief. Whenever he thought he was starting to understand the pitbull's modus operandi, the animal suddenly did something completely out of character. Sometimes he wondered if *he* was the one on the end of the psychological leash in this whole human/animal relationship.

"Just bring your bike on in here, mister. Mister?"

"Howzer," Stone lied, not wanting the old man to know who he was. It could be his life if he did.

"Well, you just bring that ol' ve-hi-cle in here." He led the way, sweeping the cobwebs out of their path from the low rafters. The place obviously hadn't been used for a long, long time. "Now, this ain't your Hilton Hotel or nothing," Pliers said, "but she's clean, no rats around here—and no leaks neither," he added proudly, pointing up at the ceiling, which, as far as Stone could see, didn't show any signs of water damage.

"Used to be a roofer, among other things," the man said boastfully. "Other people may let their houses fall down around them," he said cryptically, "but old Pliers takes care of what's his."

"Well, this will do just fine," Stone said, parking the bike behind an old stall so it wasn't visible from the front. "Just fine." He headed back out to the yard and saw Excaliber still twisting in tight little circles as the yapping little dog followed ceaselessly after him.

"Now, the only thing is," Stone went on, "is though my dog and your dog are ol' pals, usually Excaliber doesn't get on too well with other animals. Is there any kind of fence or place you could keep him sort of corraled in while I'm in town?"

"Matter of fact, I was just repairing my barbed-wire barrier," the old man replied. "It had gotten rusty, but I cut out the bad and interwove a batch of new stuff I was able to get my hands on and—" He pulled back a tarp on the ground, and Stone saw a circle of barbed wire on a long roll, ready to be pulled out. "Gotta have something around here," Pliers said, spitting out a wad of brown. "Goddamn place ain't nothing but thieves and killers, who'd rape their own grandmother if they had half a chance."

"I'm looking for Joey "Cheap" Scalzanni. Have you heard of him?" Stone asked.

"Scalzanni? Hey, mister, he's the bastard who runs the whole damn show here. *Numero uno*. Don't you know what's going on?"

"Sorry, I'm a stranger in these parts," Stone said, shrugging his shoulders. "Here . . . on business."

"Well, if you ain't one of them, I don't know what kind of business you got here. But just looking at you and seeing that you're basically a decent fellow, I'll have to tell you that if you go in there, you ain't coming back. And that being the case, I'll have to ask you for another one of the dollars for your dog there. 'Cause I'm willing to feed him, but even with these"—he jangled the coins—"a dog'll eat a hell of a lot of food over the years. And—"

"You don't have to convince me," Stone said, reaching into his jacket pocket again. This time he took out ten of the silver circles and handed them over. The old man's greedy eyes almost popped their sockets as he scooped them in toward himself, and two of them fell.

"Your dog will eat meat—every day. I swear to God. You hear me, mister." Pliers said, laughing as he dropped to his knee to collect the two errant coins. He was rich now, richer than he had ever dreamed was possible. Why, he would be able to have what he had dreamed of for years now—a hand-cranked phonograph that he had seen in the town. And records. He could listen to music again.

"Oh, God, thank you, thank you," he sputtered over and over again as he took the fortune of shimmering silver and buried it behind the barn in a foul-looking area of compost and rat corpses. No one would look there. Not even another rat.

Stone told Excaliber to stay, but the dog was so engrossed in his play that he didn't even see him. Stone knew that the animal was trained enough to stay where he left it. Besides, Pliers would doubtless serve up a feast of horse meat tonight to celebrate. That would insure the animal's sticking at home base, lying flat on its back.

Stone checked both his weapons as he walked out into the darkness again, the crickets crackling like the hills were alive with them. He had the Uzi mini-autopistol in his chest holster, and the Ruger .44 Mag at his waist. Both were fully loaded, ready to give the undertaker some overtime. He walked toward the edge of the town which was about half a mile off. Though it was barely five o'clock, the sky seemed as dark as if it were approaching midnight. The clouds above appeared swollen, ready to burst their infected guts of poison at any time. But enough light filtered over from the town so that Stone could stumble along. And as he went, he pulled a few things out from his jacket. Concepts that Dr. Kennedy had shown him when they traveled together. A disguise—how just a few things could take someone's eye off your main features. A blue wool sailor's cap and a pair of glasses, which were actually just clear glass but had suave tortoise shell rims that curled back Art Deco fashion. The cap and glasses, plus the five-day growth of stubble on his face, made him look radically different from the Martin Stone any of the bastards might have seen before. Or so he hoped.

Then he was there. There was no mistaking the fact that he had come to the town limits of Keenesburg. For like all Mafia towns, it had its own rules, its own sign of welcome —poles fifteen feet apart with human heads on them. Shrunken, shriveled, twisted little leathery coconuts of brown and black, with eyes turned to black tar the size of grapes staring down at the hesitant traveler. Telling him, "Turn around and leave now, asshole. Unless you're one tough motherfucker, you'll most likely end up on this pole with me."

Stone touched his hat as if tipping it as he walked past the cranial guardians of the place and stepped onto a cracked asphalt road. It was lighter here, as bulbs had been strung up on walls and sticks every hundred feet or so. Unadorned, almost blinding little spheres of white sent out sharp shadows from the two- and three-story buildings that lined both sides of what was apparently the main street. The buildings were all wrecks, windows gone, doors gone, whole structures tilting to one side like the Leaning Tower of Pisa. And the few people he saw sitting on rocks or on small logs in front of them looked about as wrecked as their homes. Listless eyes, jaws hanging slack. A few of them tried to talk as Stone walked along, but all he heard was gibberish. It was like a town of the mad, the brain-dead.

And *that* was one of the better sections, Stone found out as he walked on. For as he drew past the "residential" housing and more into the business section of the town, skid row appeared. Drunken, bleeding wrecks of humanity lined the streets as little concrete pillboxes dispensed shots of rotgut whiskey through their holes. In this town liquor, because of its ability to cause unconsciousness, was the most precious commodity of all. Stone saw figures leaning over the most stupefied of the fallen drunks and going through their clothes, even taking them, so that they were stripped naked. But he did nothing. He wasn't Jesus Christ.

Here and there rats peered out from rusting gratings or scampered among some of the motionless bodies that appeared to be dead. One was; Stone saw flies buzzing in and out of its mouth and nose. Then the snout of an immense rat ran out of the edge of a basement and under the corpse's shirt where it began gnawing in a frenzy, as Stone could see from the jerking movements beneath the dead man's shirt. He was going to have to try to became a travel rep for the place, Stone thought with dark humor, just to keep himself from vomiting. He knew lots of people who would just love to come here for their winter vacation.

As he went on, the bars seemed to get a little better, the clientele if not less ugly, at least able to stand up and walk around, until at last he reached what was clearly the town's crossroad. Stone came to a corner, turned, and stood frozen as he saw what lay ahead. For never in his wildest dreams had he encountered quite such a vision, quite such a darkness on the face of the earth.

Chapter Fourteen _____

S tone was staring at a shopping center of crime. A giant
mall carrying all the tools and accessories of death.
Blocks of two-storied picture windowed stores spread
off in every direction in what must have been at least a
ten-block-square setup. It didn't look all that dissimilar to a
big suburban mall of old but for one thing—what they were
selling. For as Stone walked down one of the corridors that
ran through the place, his eyes opened wide. Behind the
Plexiglas store windows were all the things a hoodlum, a
murderer, or even a full-fledged crime lord could ever want.

Racks of pistols filled one window, machine guns another. On one side two full showrooms of knives, brass
knuckles, and other hand-to-hand utensils for heavy-duty
maiming or disemboweling. Behind another window sat a
wide selection of torture items—electric prods, nooses,
chairs with spikes on them, racks, gallows. . . . All in all,
Stone could see, these bastards carried every goddamn thing
known to man for the mortification and destruction of
human flesh.

The crowds that filled the mall's walkways as Stone got
deeper into it all seemed to be absolutely entranced by the
goods on display. If Al Capone had died and gone to heaven,
he would have reappeared here, strutting along as the gang-
sters here did, in their purple and pink and black silk suits.
Scarred, smashed-in faces peered like orphans, faces pressed
against the inch-thick Plexiglas. Their lifelong dreams were

inside those displays. Garrotes, hatches, axes, poisons, bombs, gases. For those who cared, not a thing had been left out.

Stone made a right down one of the many high-ceilinged corridors that filled the place. It obviously had been a real mall once. No one could have built something like this since America had collapsed. But though they had tried to keep it up, the deterioration, the crumbling plaster, couldn't really be hidden. Patches of ceiling were falling down, the industrial rug on the floors had been meant to be changed every five years. It hadn't been touched for twelve years, cleaned for three. The dirt of tens of thousands of pairs of boots and shoes, cigarette butts, spit, snot, blood, and numerous other substances had penetrated its once lime-green coloration and turned it a ghastly brownish shade, like mud.

Still, what was left was unquestionably impressive. Just the fact that the place was wired and most of its lights and neons were still working was in this day and age an achievement of some magnitude. Stone realized that he was entering a new section of the mall as women replaced weapons behind the windows. Young, beautiful women, naked for the all the world to see—and trying to lure all passersby into their lair, to give them "the Ultimate Pleasure." Each was a specialist in some aspect of the myriad ways that the human body could "play"—from straight sex, to whips, to S&M and bondage to—for those who could pay—the ultimate sex games where death itself was the object of the players' affections. Where sexual release itself was predicated on the murder of another. The sickest of the sick in a sick world.

Stone walked for nearly twenty minutes and still didn't see the same thing twice. But no April. He didn't even know exactly what he was looking for, but he knew he'd know when he found it. He saw a large neon-lit bar—The Hot Load—sandwiched between some of the sex establishments. He walked in and was met by a virtual explosion of noise, laughter, yelling voices. The place was big and filled with bastards, men with faces that looked like they had had plastic surgery performed on them by gorillas. The huge sons of bitches were loaded down with weapons like they were mobile armories—pistols of every make and function-

ing order, SMG's, shotguns, even grenades, and each man
was draped with belts of slugs to make sure he had enough
ammo to kill wholesale.

The Hot Load was basically one long bar that ran the
whole side of the joint, perhaps fifty round tables in the
middle, and then various amusements—jukeboxes, slot ma-
chines, and sluts strutting their wares on little runways,
bumping and grinding with profound crudeness along the
other wall. Stone made his way over to the bar and managed
to elbow his way gently between two lugs the size of trees.
It was another story catching the barkeep's eye as the man
was injecting himself with some substance he had secreted
just beneath the counter. But when the seven-foot and still
counting bartender finished the injection, he got a flushed,
stupid smile on his face and turned back to tend his wards.

"Whiskey," Stone said, raising his finger to catch the
man's attention. The huge fellow walked over to Stone,
squinting a little as he came. He stopped right in front of his
would-be client and stared at Stone as a drugged smile wriggled back and forth across the Neanderthal face.

"What the hell do you want, turkey?" the barkeep asked,
slurring his words so that spittle flowed out the right corner
of his mouth like a little fountain of white.

"I want—want a drink," Stone said apologetically as he
raised his shoulders slightly. His disguise, the dumb wool
hat, and the glasses made him out to be a nerd, he knew, and
he played it to the hilt. There was no way in hell any of the
slime would connect the man who had taken out a decent
number of their own with this jocko who was in the wrong
place.

"Does your mama know you're out, boy?" the barkeep
asked, unable to keep the stupid little smile from his thick
lips. He was stoned out of his mind and was getting kicks
from playing with the asshole.

"My mama?" Stone asked, a little confused as he adjusted
his wool cap slightly. "What does she have to do with—"

"You know, you're just about the stupidest asshole I've
ever seen," the man said, fixing Stone with his dark little
eyes, all lit up and swirling with the drug he had injected
into his veins. "I can't hardly believe you're still alive, ass-

hole. But I guess that Big Scumbag in the sky in his fucked-
up wisdom protects even the jerk-offs of the world."

"Well put," Stone said with an idiotic smile, adjusting his
glasses, which kept trying to fall off the tip of his nose.
Another of Dr. Kennedy's little tips. Play the fool. It will
make other men feel superior to you and consequently keep
you around just to get their rocks off.

"Well put?" the barkeep said, shaking his head in disbelief. "I insult the guy right to his fucking face and he
thanks me." He was talking back to Stone, but it was as if he
were addressing a third person who had nothing to do with
what was going on. "Can you believe that shit? Jeez!" He
threw his head back to laugh, and stuff flew out of his nose
and mouth.

"Well, you see—" Stone said, starting to explain why he
appreciated the truthfulness and directly expressed words of
the fellow when the man's face snapped back down out of its
other wordly trips.

"Shut up, asshole," the barkeep said with an almost be-
nevolent grin on his face. Now that he had decided not to
kill the little twerp himself, the bartender had taken a sort of
liking to the turd and felt protective toward him. "Whiskey,
you say. Then whiskey it shall be." He reached behind him
and pulled a bottle down from the shelf, then reached down,
extracted a filthy, grease-coated glass and filled it to the brim
so it was flowing over the sides.

"Here you go, asshole," he said, holding it out with a
suddenly lurching jerk of his arm so that about a third of the
drink sloshed onto Stone's jacket.

"Uh, thanks," Stone said, taking it and gulping down a
few quick drafts. It was wretched, horrible stuff, but he
could taste the alcohol somewhere within it, which gave a
pleasant burning sensation to his throat and chest, warming
him momentarily from the cold.

"So what's a little snail like you doing here?" the barkeep
asked after he had put back the bottle. He sipped a blue
liquid from his own little glass, which brought a happy smile
to his lips every time he took a toot on it. To affect a moose
like that, Stone knew, the shit must be hot enough to power
rockets.

"Well," Stone said, talking in a slow, annoying, high-pitched tonality. "Me dad just died—bless his soul—and now that I'm a man of some means . . ." He raised himself up an inch or two and pulled up the waist of his pants as if he were hot shit. Which just added to the bartender's amusement, as he could see by the cheap duds the turd was wearing that he was from the lowest of the low.

"Yeah, yeah," the barkeep said impatiently. "Talk faster, asshole." He leaned over on the long oak bar and looked menacingly at Stone.

"Well, yes—you see—of course," Stone stuttered, playing his role for all it was worth, "the point is, I'm here to get me a woman. A wife, that is. Or maybe—two of 'em, if I can afford it." He stared over at the baseball-mitt-sized, acned face of the bartender with wide eyes like a teenager about to lose his virginity.

"Jesus Christ," the barkeep said, slapping his hand over his own forehead in bemused exasperation. "I know you were a turd and an asshole—but I didn't realize you were a fucking moron too," the man said, standing up tall so that he towered over Stone. "And just how much was you 'specting to spend for these two bitches of yours, Mr. Rich Turd?"

"Sky's the limit with me," Stone said grandiosely, sweeping his hand like a windshield wiper in front of him. "Just sold some cows, even a horse," Stone confided to the guy. "Don't tell anyone—cause I kin trust you," Stone went on, leaning forward himself, "but I gots me nearly fifty dollars here in my boot to buy me some woman meat." Stone laughed as if he were trying to be lewd and lascivious, but it came out like Jerry Lewis having a coughing spell.

"Good god," the man said with a sigh, crossing himself three times, which Stone found to be quite an odd gesture, considering that the man worked in perhaps the most evil, most perverted drug and sex operation on the planet. "Fifty fucking dollars, huh?" He paused for a moment and put his hand beneath his chin as if considering the whole affair with great deliberation. Then he looked back at Stone with utmost sincerity and said, "Then I think you better head over to the pigpens at the north end of town—buy yourself a sow, boy. Give her some of your rod, and I'm sure you could get a whole damn stable of little porkers oinking all over the fucking place."

"You mean, I—I won't be able to afford a breeding bitch with fifty dollars?" Stone asked, crestfallen. "It seemed like so much when I—I got it."

"Listen, stupid. I don't know why the hell I'm even talking to you—maybe because you remind me of my dead brother, Tino, he had glasses like you—but if I were you, I'd just forget about getting me a woman right now. Even the cheapest of 'em—and I'm not talking about fresh meat from the country that ain't even been used up or anything—but even old whores, fifty-year-olds with tits hanging down to their toes and bashed-in faces from ten thousand bangs up their cazooties. Even them asshole—they start at a hundred. You hear what I'm saying? You're out of the market."

"Damn," Stone said, punching one hand into the palm of the other. "I had it all figured out—where she'd put her little things and—"

"Jesus Christ." The barkeep groaned. Each time he thought he had gauged the turkey's brain level, the turd did something to drop it even lower. "Forget it, asshole," the tender said. "That shit ain't for you. Just spend your money here. Drink, shoot up, get a whore, and fuck her till your brains come out of your ears. Party like a maniac for one night—and then go back to your farm and screw your animals. And if you're real lucky one day, one of them might just give birth to something that was half animal and half asshole. And that, my stupid friend, would be a sight to see." He smiled at Stone, who acted like he didn't quite know if he had just been complimented or insulted, but he took another slug of the rotten rotgut.

Suddenly there was a commotion off toward the center of the bar, and Stone saw the barkeep's eyes light up like warning flashers on a radar tracker. With one hand on the wood top, the bartender leapt in a single jump up and over the bar, down onto the floor, and through the crowd—all in the space of about a second. Stone was amazed by the man's speed. For someone that size, he moved like a cat. Stone made a mental note: If ever—God help him—he went up against the son of a bitch, he'd remember to use a gun—or a bazooka, preferably.

Stone followed quickly behind, using the space the bartender had forged through the still half-sprawled men who had been knocked aside for thirty feet or so to where the commotion was taking place. Stone stepped to the very edge of the crowd, which had cleared back so that a rough square about ten feet on a side had been created. Two men faced each other with murder in their eyes. One was huge—perhaps even larger than the bartender—with an immense coat that covered him from shoulder to floor and was made of skunk skins sewn crudely together. The effect of black-and-white stripes all over the huge body, moving and undulating as their wearer did, was striking. Facing him, about six feet away, was a much smaller and leaner man. And meaner-looking by far. His face was thin and narrow like a rodent's, all the skin stretched back taut and tight so the front of it almost seemed to come to a point. And with his greased-back, slick black hair, which lay like a sheen of ink over his head, the impression created of some sort of filthy, sewage-coated rat was quite strong—to Stone's eyes, at least.

The two adversaries tried to stare each other down, but the smaller man was winning, as his steely eyes bore into the larger one, so that the huge skunk-clad mountain man stepped back a few inches, dizzy.

"Boss, boss, you want me to help you?" the huge barkeep screamed out, standing just at the edge of the crowd of fur- and leather-coated men who stood, drinks in hand, and watched it all, hoping some blood would be shed on this otherwise boring evening.

"No, stay back," the ratlike man replied with icy command in his voice. He wore an all black suit, black tie, shirt; every goddamn thing on the man was black. And as he circled slowly around his huge challenger he threw the lower flaps of his silk jacket back away from his hips.

"I don't care if you are Joey Scalzanni himself," the mountain boy said with a sneer, suddenly regaining his courage after turning away from the little man's eyes for a few seconds, "you took my fucking money—and I want it back." He reached inside his coat and took out a handcrafted knife that must have run two feet long from hilt to blade tip. Stone thought he had seen big blades before, but this thing looked like it could take out an elephant.

"Took *your* money?" Scalzanni laughed, a nasty little sound from hell. "I wouldn't touch your stinking money with a ten-foot pole," the weasel of a man spat out in disgust. Both of his arms whipped out in a blur from his coat, and suddenly two hooks were clutched in each claw of a hand. Meat hooks—long and curved, ready to sink into huge cattle carcasses and move them along. What they could do to a man, Stone didn't want to think about. So this was Scalzanni—the son of a bitch who had killed Doc Kennedy or ordered it, and had had April kidnapped. He could see the family resemblance between this one and the brother of the man, who Stone had taken out months before. They both looked like rats. And both experts in hand weapons. The other man had handled knives like he was a chef in a sushi bar. And this one handled the meat hooks like a seasoned butcher. By the way he moved gingerly around the barroom floor, by the way a smile like a fresh gash worked its way in sadistic expectation across Scalzanni's face, by the way he slowly turned the huge hooks in his small hands, Stone knew he was about to witness a massacre.

And he didn't have to wait long. For suddenly, with a roar befitting his mighty stature and small brain, the huge mountain man, who apparently believed that Joey "Cheap" Scalzanni, the owner of The Hot Load and half the buildings and whores in town, had defrauded him of a hundred dollars' worth of hides the week before, lunged forward slashing the blade of his great beheader down like he was ready to slice through trees. But Scalzanni, hardly 5'5", 120 pounds of amphetamine-crazed, psychotic energy, danced back on his toes, letting out horrible little giggles as his eyes lit up.

"Come on, dinosaur, I heard you were tough. I think you're just homoshit, you hear me?" Scalzanni made a clicking sound with his teeth and tongue and waved his fingers forward. The gesture infuriated the skunk-clad attacker, and his face turned beet-red. With another roar, totally forgetting who or where he was, the bear of a man rushed forward in one huge arcing step, slashing four times back and forth in the air at the Mafia warlord.

But somehow Scalzanni wasn't there. Again with that spine-scraping giggle, he danced down real low on his toes and shot right around the slashing giant. He came up and spun on one of his shiny, pointed Italian shoes, circa 1950s, and whipped his right hand around in a blur. The hook ripped into the man's side, digging clear into his lungs and sternum. Scalzanni gripped hard around the wooden handle and pulled back with all his might. Ripping muscle and lungs and every damn thing inside, the steel hook spun the mountain man completely around like a top just released from its string.

Only what this top of human flesh found on its first half revolution was revolting to the max, for Scalzanni's other hand came up with the speed of a leopard's paw and the chromed hook, kept all bright and shining as if it were the new chromium bumpers on a Caddy, tore through the lug's face like a scythe. The mountain man, who had been in mid-yowl from the terrible pain of the first wound, as half his lungs were dripping out, suddenly heard his vocal cords sending out a scream of pure terror as he saw the point of the hook coming right toward his eye.

The ice-pick sharp tip of the long question mark of steel dug into the eye, then the brain, then the back of the skull. With a sharp shriek of delight Scalzanni pulled back hard, and the hook ripped forward again a few inches, pulling out a geyser of mush and slime from the eye socket and nose of the struggling mountain man. He flopped around as Scalzanni held him on his toes, one hook through his eye and brain, the other all the way inside his chest—like a double-hooked fish out of water, gasping frantically for oxygen, though each time he exhaled, a big gush of blood spurted out.

The Mafia boss led the wretched thing around the center of the circle as the crowd pulled back so as not to get their fancy town duds all bloody. The little rat of a killer was in his element now, knowing how to play with the crowds to the utmost. He had started out, after all, as had all his brothers, all seven of them, only five now left, as shills—

selling shoddy goods and bad drugs in the dark back streets of America. He had worked his way up through a sea of blood, treachery, and assassination. And even now that he was at the very top of his profession—a don of dons, one of the Council of Twelve who divvied up the pie that was the collapsed America—still, he liked to put on a show for the common asshole every now and again.

Among the many things that the black-suited Mafia king had been in his early days was a butcher. He had worked in a stockyard in Chicago where he had handled the big dumb steers, their throats freshly slit, had poked and pulled them along with two such meat hooks. And he had gotten to be an expert with the things, able to manipulate, move along even tons of meat with the expertise of a surgeon. Thus it was little effort for him to turn and spin the wretched piece of humanity he had caught in his hooks. He walked the bloody, spurting thing, which gasped out bubbles, perhaps some last farewell or prayer, though all that came out was a foam of red that dribbled down his chin like a baby that had eaten too much jelly.

Scalzanni completed one complete turn of the square of combat created by the surrounding crowd around the wide-planked wooden floor. When he had gotten back to roughly where he had started, he stopped and bent down with his knees so the flopping man's knees lowered, too, as he followed his manipulator like a puppet on strings of pain. Then with a burst of energy that startled Stone, who was right in front of all the action, just a yard away on one side of the crowd, Scalzanni stood up fast and swung his arms up with all his might. All 350 pounds plus of dumb Rocky Mountain fur trapper shot up into the air like a shell being launched from a cannon. Only this shell was made of flesh and blood. As it left the floor, Scalzanni ripped backward on the hooks with a snap of his hands, and they pulled free of the body. The force of the dual motion was incredible, sending the body both flying up into the air a good eight feet off the ground and at the same time ripping it apart as the hooks tore free. The head just seemed to explode out, the skull and brain tissue, along with a single eyeball, spiraled out into the air, while from below the lungs and ribs all snapped apart like a smashed wall of lathing and tumbled into the air.

The red meteor of flesh flew perhaps fifteen feet before it crashed down right on top of, and then through, a table. It slammed onto the floor headfirst—or what was left of it—though that, too, splattered into a coarse pulp. The rest of the huge body followed right behind and came to a flopping rest on the floor. The thing just lay there, twitching and jerking like wild. Death had come so fast and so painfully that it didn't even quite realize that it no longer existed. That it was not human any longer but a mockery of a man. A carving of death, an artwork of mutilation.

The crowd edged in closer, all talking at once as laughter and screams of madness echoed through The Hot Load. They all wanted a view, and numerous fights broke out as every son of a bitch in the place fought for an up-close visual inspection of the monstrosity that twitched and spasmed its way out of this life and into the next black pit that awaited it.

Chapter Fifteen _____

"**D**rinks on the house," Scalzanni screamed in that same shrill voice, like a rat in a sewer squeaking out that it had just killed something that stupidly had passed by. "I always feels generous right after I has killed," the Mafia chieftain said, waving his hand toward the bar. The man right in front of Stone, a prospector with a football helmet on his head and 12-gauge pump shotgun around his shoulder, turned suddenly to get his free booze and came barreling toward Stone, wanting to be the first at the bar. He raised his elbow as he stepped forward to level the spectacled nerd before him. But the elbow never reached Stone's face.

Without a chance to realize he was going out of character, Stone swung his head down and below the man's incoming elbow, and in a blur swung his hand in a blade up and into the man's groin from below. The gold miner turned green and blue and shot backward, as if he'd just bounced off a wall. The gasping miner collapsed in a heap just a foot or so behind Scalzanni's back. Still motioning for the masses to head on over to the free drinks, the Mafia chief jerked around on a dime and snapped both arms out at shoulder length, ready to pinion anything that was between the two hooks like a butterfly under glass.

As he twisted his head around, the sprawled prospector saw what was awaiting him and let out an imploring wail.

"Don't kill me, boss," the man pleaded through broken

teeth. "It was him what pushed me." He pointed a filthy, accusing finger at Stone, who stood in what suddenly felt like a very naked position at the edge of the crowd. Stone fell right back into his dumb character praying that no one had seen the fast move. He wished now that he'd taken the goddamn blow. He sure as hell wasn't ready to have it out with this little meat-hook master here in his own place—with five hundred other psychos surrounding him who would just as soon rip his balls off.

"Gosh," Stone said, stuttering and fixing his glasses. "I sure am sorry that man tried to attack you." Stone added a few nervous tics on his cheeks and eyes just for good measure. "But I sure as heck didn't push a tough fella like that." He pointed down at the gray-bearded, buffalo-hided prospector, who didn't dare raise himself up, as he was afraid Scalzanni would make instant burger of him if he moved an inch. The Mafia chief stared over at Stone, then back at the man on the floor. Then his eyes went back to Stone again, and he seemed to be studying him closely for seconds. Stone could feel the dark little rat eyes trying to bore into him, and he just kept the stupid grin of confusion on his face and tipped his glasses again so they almost fell off the end of his nose.

"Bah," Scalzanni spat suddenly, turning and walking away as he spun the two meat hooks around in his bony hands and then deposited them in a flash back inside their hidden holsters, which hung on each hip inside his oversize black silk jacket. He had already killed a huge son of a bitch—it would be anticlimactic to trifle with these two peons. Boring as well, which was even worse. The Mafia lord walked toward the bar with both hands on his hips as the crowd, even in its confusion, cleared a Red Sea for the man. All of them, being cutthroats, rapists, and killers themselves, admired Scalzanni greatly, but being mortal men, they gave him a wide berth, at least wide enough so that if he whipped out those little hooks of instant death, they'd be out of his range—for a second or two, anyway.

Stone quickly turned as Scalzanni walked off and blended into the crowd as it surged to the opposite side of the room. He had scarcely gone five feet, looking quickly around to make sure no one else had their eye on him, when he felt another elbow hook onto his arm and start to pull him. Stone turned, his fist cocked, ready to smash someone right in the throat. But he held it suspended in midair when he saw a woman alongside him, smiling up as sweetly as any spider ever did to any fly.

"Going my way, cutie?" the woman asked as she continued to half drag Stone along. He quickly lowered his fist, realizing it looked a little ridiculous just hanging up there. As she pulled him deeper into the recesses of the bar, a squad of cleanup men came running out with body bag and shovels to cart away the early refuse of the evening. But there would be more.

"Come on, junior." The B-girl laughed as she pulled him past the four-deep crowd, which now lined the entire length of the bar, cashing in on Scalzanni's offer. "You don't want to go hang out with this bunch. Why, they'll eat you alive." As they passed beneath one of the dozen half-shattered chandeliers that hung from the ceiling, Stone got a good look at her as she pushed some half-dozing drunks out of the way. She had been beautiful—once. There were still traces of it—somewhere. The skin of her forehead was still an ivory white, a sign of what had once been. The eyes, blue and intelligent, danced in her face. But the rest of the face was a mask of lines—of a thousand grimaces and tears that had dug valleys down every side—and the covering creases. A nose that had been shattered, an ear badly infected—and covered with a pink rash. She looked like she had been through and seen everything—and now to cover it all up, since she was still a "working girl," the woman had covered up the damage with industrial-strength pancake makeup, lipstick, rouge, eyeliner—and every other damn thing she could get her hands on. Her hand, which rested on Stone's right arm as she dragged him along in a crude but effective sort of arm lock, had bright purple fingernails as long as claws, and they followed the curve of Stone's sleeve as if he were in the grip of a man-eater.

"There, there, isn't that better," she said with a smile, her apple-red lips made up in Kewpie-doll style so they appeared tiny and scrunched together, just ready for kissing.

She dragged him out of the main bar and into another room in the back. Stone allowed himself to be guided along, as he felt it was to his physical benefit to get away from Scalzanni for the moment, that is, he didn't feel like dying right now.

"Yes, much," Stone said with his doofus grin again, patting her hand reassuringly as they stepped into the smaller and more dimly lit playroom. "You're so kind," Stone went on. "I was just so—lost in there. I—I—don't have any friends in town and—" He wrinkled his nose as if he might sneeze. A strong whiff of her numerous cheap and overdosed perfumes filled his nose like he was standing over the smokestack of a chemical plant.

"Ah, don't you now?" The whore cackled with a look of twisted concern so that her eyes, which were lined with blue and pink and orange and so many other colors that it appeared more as if she had been trying to paint Easter eggs than apply makeup around them, rolled back and floated around in her head. "Well, you've come to the right damn place, then, mister. Mister—"

"Mulganey." Stone grinned back, poking at his glasses so they popped up off one ear. "Here—looking for—" He glanced shyly at her for a second, and then boldly went on, "For a breeding bitch."

"Oh, how romantic," the whore said, slapping herself with her free hand in the cheek, the strike being a little harder than she had intended, and it sent up a big puff of the quarter-inch-thick pancake makeup into the air in a smoke ring. "How romantic. Isn't this just my night. I'm Peaches. Peaches and Cream, but my friends"—she looked at Stone and batted her eyes a number of times very fast, their long, fake lashes extending over them like canopies—"call me Peaches. Oh, you and I are going to have a lot of fun tonight, aren't we, my little snookums pie."

"Gee, I sure hope so," Stone answered, pulling his lips back as he glanced at her to reveal his toothiest and perhaps stupidest grin. He heard a splashing sound and dragged her slightly in that direction a few yards to take a look. A swimming pool about forty feet long and twenty wide was filled with young naked women. Perhaps two dozen of them. They scampered and jumped around in the water, splashed and squealed as they tried to—or pretended to—get away from the ropes that were being tossed at them constantly. For around the pool stood a crowd of men—bikers, Mafia middle management, free-lance killers and assassins, even just run-of-the-mill mountain bandits here for a holiday—all holding fishing rods as thick as baseball bats with thick steer-roping lariats hanging from the ends. Every rope had a pre-tied lasso on the end with a slipknot so it would pull closed in a second once it reached its target.

Even while Stone watched, two of the fishermen got lucky, and their ropes landed cleanly around two of the whore-mermaids. They were pulled, kicking and squealing like stuck pigs, from the water and lowered over onto the floor where their captors grabbed them with gusto. All kinds of noises and sounds ensued.

"Quite amazing," Stone mumbled with true incredulity. "I bet they have a 'whale' of a good time, huh?" He grinned at her and then winked to show he'd made, or had attempted to make, a joke.

"Oh, yes—whale of a time. Yes, that's really good." She smiled at him through huge red lips. "You're a scream, junior, a real scream." She turned her face away from him for a moment and silently mouthed the word *asshole* to her own private entities.

"Well, at least you can talk," she said, looking back upon him fondly. "That's a good start. You should see some of them around here." She shook her hand back and forth.

"Oh, yes, I can talk real good," Stone said animatedly. "I've talked all my life. Why, I can talk about all kinds of things."

"Yes—that's—that's great, Mulganey," Peaches said, patting his hand sympathetically as she pulled him toward a series of darkened booths inside of which Stone could see couples grinding away and making licky-face as they prepared for quick departures to the nearby bedrooms.

"Here, we'll be much cozier in here. Yes, yes." She patted his head, half pushing Stone down into the seat as she got in on the other side of the table with a thud. Before they had even touched the leather of the seat, a waitress, her breasts bare, the rest of her clad in just a loincloth in the shape of a skull and crossbones, came over for their orders.

"Champagne," Peaches said, looking up at the waitress as she winked her eye. "Right, Mulganey? Only the best for us."

"Gosh darn right," Stone said, slamming his fist down toward the table but catching it at the last second so it hardly made a sound as it reached the wood. "Only the best for me and my gal." He smiled at Peaches, who reached across the table with a snakelike hand, searching for his hand. When she found it, she clamped down hard like a cobra swallowing a mouse and nailed him to the table. The woman had learned all the moves. Every damn one of them.

"So tell me all about yourself, snookums," Peaches said, leaning forward in the half-darkness, illuminated only by candlelit lanterns hanging here and there on the walls. She batted her huge eyelashes, which must have come out a good two inches from her eyes, curving off in both directions like Bambi's lashes rather than those of a sixty-year-old whore with five diseases, two of them fatal.

Stone had just drawn in his breath to say something dumb when his eyes adjusted to the dimness of the room and he saw something ten yards off that nearly made his heart stop in his chest. It was a man and a woman, naked, standing fact-to-face, perhaps eight inches apart. And even through the darkness it was instantly clear to Stone that they were dead. The pallor to their skin, their facial features hanging like a piece of dough left on the edge of a table. The purple, swollen fingers and feet was where all the blood had accumulated. And as Stone watched, wondering if he had fallen into a nightmare, he realized that the two of them were moving, moving in relation to each other. And suddenly he saw that the organ of the male cadaver has been placed into the entrance of the female. And that, though dead, the two were fucking.

As his eyes adjusted more, Stone could see the dim outlines of frames of wire and metal stuck into the things from behind, making them move. When he was younger, he remembered seeing coin-operated booths at county fairs where mechanical figures had moved, danced, boxed with each other. They must have gotten hold of some of them—and modified them slightly.

"Oh, are you looking at Matilda and Fred?" the whore asked him with a cheery smile as she sprayed a little mist from an atomizer onto her neck and face so that the booth felt like it had just been gassed. "Aren't they the greatest?" She laughed. "They're the talk of the whole territory, you know. Of course, they rot after a few days. Really, the stench can get unbearable if there aren't fresh replacements to throw up there. But fortunately," she said reassuringly to him as she squeezed his hand hard, "there are lots of avail-able volunteers these days."

"That is reassuring," Stone said as he continued to stare at the copulating corpses in repulsed, but unswaying, fascination. Their hands as well had been wired up so that they almost appeared to be stroking each another, and their faces and neck, too, must have had rods implanted within them, for they seemed to turn and brush lips every few seconds like a set of those kissing dolls that Stone had always hated. Their hips thrust forward almost at the same time, slamming together with loud, squishy thwacks, the unmistakable sound that dead flesh makes when it slaps against the same. The male corpse's organ, which had set into rigor mortis, had been fit right into the female's sex opening so that it slammed in and out of her every few seconds. Whether or not they felt pleasure—what is the sensation of a dead penis fucking?—only a Zen Buddhist, a master of the highest achievement and understanding, could answer. A single blue filtered light illuminated the couple from above so that their ghostly color was even more exaggerated, their eyes spark-ling with four blue flames, as if the trapped souls within were looking back out from hell.

"Very entertaining," Stone said, turning away at last as he felt his stomach do a few funny flips and make some noises. He hoped he didn't lose it.

"Yes, isn't it, though?" Peaches grinned in the darkness, and her red lips shone like little overripe strawberries in the candlelight. "The guy who runs this place—that Scalzanni fellow who you saw out front, with the hooks. Remember—

the hooks?" She squeezed his hands again, and Stone winced.

"Oh, yeah—the hook guy. Tough—very tough. I wouldn't want to—"

"Well, he's the one who had them put in," Peaches said, cutting him off. "Great sense of humor, the guy has. I mean, what a joker, huh? Ah, here's our drinks." The aging whore cackled, rubbing her hands together as the waitress deposited a gallon bottle of "champagne" on the table and poured them each a glass. The liquid bubbled as it went into the glass, but when Stone toasted with the whore and lifted his dirt-smeared glass to his lips, he could instantly taste that it was the same rotgut he had bought at the bar—but with some CO_2 pumped into it to give it a bubbling action. It tasted foul, undrinkable.

"Drink up. Drink up, snookums," Peaches went on, her Cheshire cat of a grin undulating in the half-darkness, the red lips grinding together like worms humping in the soil. "Drink up. Tonight we party, for tomorrow we die." She laughed with fake abandon, holding her lips far apart so she didn't smear them, forming them into an *O* shape, in what appeared quite an obscene—and suggestive—gesture.

Stone took another slug of the rotgut and suddenly started feeling funny. He didn't drink a hell of a lot. But he knew he could hold his damn liquor. But as she talked to him her whole face started looking even stranger, getting all skinny, then fat again, until he felt like he was walking inside a fun-house mirror. Her words turned into a buzz of bees, and he couldn't understand a thing she was saying.

Then everything was spinning around him much too fast, and even as he rose to his feet in a futile effort to fight back, Stone realized that he had been drugged. But by then it was too late. For suddenly he was dropping, as if his legs had just been chopped off at the knees. He dimly wondered if his nose would smash into jelly when he hit face first on the floor, which was looming up at him like a locomotive coming down the track. But his brain tumbled into darkness before he even got the chance to find out.

Chapter Sixteen _____

When Stone woke up, he felt like his head had just been used as a bowling ball in the U.S. Championships.

"Jesus," he heard his own lips mumble, and even that sounded like a bomb going off an inch from his ear. He suddenly realized he was alive when he should be dead, when he had expected to be dead. Stone forced his eyes apart, seeing as the flood of light exploded into his sockets like razors slicing across the pupils that he shouldn't have done so. He slammed them shut again before he could even see what was out there, and let out an involuntary groan.

"Easy, junior, easy," a voice said from out of the painful darkness. "Just take it real easy. I'm whipping up a brew that should help counteract some of that potion you took. We Mickey Finned you," Peaches went on, and Stone heard her shuffling around on the other side of his closed eyelids. "I was supposed to kill you," she said with a giggle. "You don't know how lucky you are, boy—that you ended up in Peaches's arms and not some other bitch who would have followed orders and taken you out like an ant."

"What the hell are you talk—" Stone started to ask, forgetting that his head felt like the inside of a punching bag.

"Easy, I said," the voice from out of the darkness scolded him. "Aren't you going to listen to your Auntie Peaches? Don't you know how many men I've Mickey Finned in my time? And still, you don't want to listen to me. Ah—men," she said with half-real, half-mocking disgust. There was a rush of air toward him, and Stone could smell her strong perfumes wafting down all around him. A hand suddenly gripped him behind the neck, lifting his head up to a glass.

"Here, drink this, Mr. Martin Stone," she said, pushing him to take the liquid in. Stone nearly gagged as he heard his name spoken. That plus the fact that she had just fed him knockout drops and now was trying to get him to sip yet another beverage.

"Drink it," she said, squeezing his neck. "If I wanted to kill you, for chrissake, I could have done it anytime in the last five hours you've been out. This stuff will help you, I swear it." It made at least minimal sense to Stone, and in his present head-throbbing state, he was ready to take anything that offered help. So he sipped down the cool liquid, which didn't taste half bad once he got over his trepidations that he was drinking his last. And lo and behold, within only minutes he was sitting up and able to talk without the reverberations slamming back and forth inside his skull.

"Okay, thanks," Stone said. He no longer had his wool cap or glasses on anymore, and he didn't look for them. She knew who he was. "Now tell me what the hell is going on," he said, propped up on the pillow as she stood at the far end of the bed, her hands draped over a wooden footboard. "First you Mickey Finned me, then you were supposed to kill me, then you didn't kill me, then—"

"You were designated a Mark Three," Peaches said, cutting him off with a curt smack of her plump, blood-red lips.

"A what?" Stone asked, rubbing his temples with the palms of his hands, trying to get the sensation of tightness out of his skull.

"A Mark Three. Everyone who comes in the place, the back room, anyway, the 'take room,' as we call it, for 'take the suckers off,' is given a number that identifies him as either a Mark One, don't touch because he's too important; Mark Two, who can be drugged and ripped off but then just thrown out of the place, and a Mark Three, who is clearly a geek of highest order—without friends in high or even low places. He is to be killed and stripped of everything—even gold or silver teeth. That was to be your fate, Mr. Stone."

"So how come I'm not dead?" Stone asked as he took little sips of the cool amber liquid she had given him. It seemed to make everything a hell of a lot better, sending streams of cooling comfort through his burning veins.

"Because I decided not to kill you, that's why," Peaches said, staring Stone right in the eye from the other end of the bed. "You don't remember me," the ancient whore went on, "but I was one of the slaves from the Dwarf's mansion—the Last Resort. We were being brought in on a truck just as you were fleeing the place. You took the diesel and drove us the hell out, just as the whole damn resort blew its stack straight to hell. We helped dig you out from the debris afterward. Anyway, I told you—you wouldn't remember. I was just one of twenty dirty whores in the darkness."

"I—I—" Stone started to stutter, not remembering her at all from the group of grime-coated, smock-clad women who had helped him but not wanting to say it.

"Oh, shut up, you have no reason to remember me, so don't apologize. You're lapsing into your dumb-asshole routine. Perhaps it's become permanent." Stone chuckled at the nasty comment. The women had a biting way with words that got right under your skin.

"I knew it was you right when I latched on to you on the bar floor, Stone. I saw how you handled that bazooka who tried to elbow your face to the wall. No one else did, but I did. I always got my eye on things. You're damn lucky Scalzanni didn't see it—he's as sharp as a fucking razor, believe it. But his back was turned. I had heard they'd set some kind of trap or something for somebody. The bigwigs had been talking about it to each other for days, and some of the other girls had heard a thing or two. So I put two and two together—and ol' Peaches 'n' Cream walks over and just delivers your smooth little ass right out of the clutches of the devil. I had to Finn you—'cause everyone keeps an eye on the operation. Then when you passed out, two of the waiters helped me carry you up to the room here. Then I was supposed to strip you, take everything worth taking, including, as I mentioned, your gold teeth. When we off someone, Scalzanni gives us ten percent of everything we collect. He's very generous. Guess he figures we'll search a little deeper, if you know what I mean."

"How would you have done it?" Stone gulped, realizing for the first time just how incredibly close to death he had been only minutes before.

"Oh, simple, we don't even mess the place up." She pulled out a long ice pick a good fourteen inches in length and as thin as a beam of light. "Just turn the unconscious mark on his stomach, insert this at the base of the neck, press it in, then twist it around like this a few times"—she turned the pick in the air as if slicing through nerve cells—"and that's that. Severs the spinal chord at its narrowest and most vulnerable part. So easy. I can't understand why everybody doesn't kill like that. All that blood is so unnecessary."

"And how often does this go on? This ice picking?" Stone asked in disgust.

"Oh, three, four, five—I don't know, maybe up to eight a day, if there's a big crowd."

"And nobody misses them?" Stone asked, amazed at the scope of the operation, though not particularly misty-eyed over the demise of the kind of shopper who came here.

"You see the scum we got in Keenesburg." Peaches laughed with a snort of ultimate disdain. "These morons can hardly wipe their behinds. A lot of them are loners up in the mountains. Or gunslingers just roaming around trying to drum up some business. These guys get killed, disappear all the time. Nobody misses them. Nobody even notices them."

"And the bodies?" Stone asked as he finished off the last of the brain-clearing brew and wished he had more. He was just starting to feel vaguely human.

"Oh, they're taken away in the dumbwaiters we have here. Every room has one." She walked over to the wall and opened a small door, revealing a shaftway with ropes hanging in it. "They're lowered down to the subbasement and taken in wheelbarrows to the pit at the far end of the mall, way in the back where they don't let anybody go. I hate it back there," the powder-coated whore said with a shiver. "It's like a swamp and a sewer and a graveyard all mixed together. It's black and horrible. They just throw the bodies in one after another, then they pour acids and lyes over everything, so the whole place just keeps filling up—and melting away with the dead bodies. You can—can even see bits of them floating around—legs, arms, heads. They come up sometimes and—"

Peaches stopped in mid-sentence and looked truly pale. It was the first time Stone had seen her show even a hint of emotion or weakness. It made him trust her just a little more that such a thing could sicken her.

"Anyway, I had killed one lover boy already, but that didn't bother me too much—the world is a better place without him—I guarantee you. But you—you was supposed to be my second. And I couldn't—just couldn't. 'Specially after you saved my damn ass. I'd just be part of the rubble back there at the Last Resort but for you—even if you did blow the place up."

"Well, I sure appreciate your not sticking that ice pick in my neck," Stone said, rubbing it. "It's sore enough already."

"Why are you here?" she asked, suddenly moving toward him so that she was leaning over the bed, and her watermelon-sized breasts squeezed forward in her taffeta body dress as if they were about to explode out at any second.

"My sister," Stone said as he drained the last drop of the restorative liquid and sat up looking around for his weapons. As soon as he could walk straight, he had to get going. This place was hell on earth. God only knew what was happening to her at this very moment. "They killed a good man I knew —Dr. Kennedy—and took my sister, April. 'Brought her to Keenesburg'—those were Kennedy's dying words.

"They squashed the Snakeman," Peaches said, her face going even paler under the pancake, the lips dry under the greasy red lipstick. "I knew the doc good, real good. He treated some of the girls at various places I've 'worked' over the years. He was a good man—like you say, Stone, a good man. They took out the doc." She shook her head back and forth, like a little girl who's just seen Santa shot and the Easter Bunny tortured and castrated. She'd seen a lot, to say the least. More than most people could if they lived to be a thousand. And most of what she'd seen had been bad, real bad. Yet still, within her sarcastic tongue and cynical core there dwelt a microscopic flower of hope and love. And Dr.

Kennedy had filled a big place there. One of the few who had actually wanted to help her.

"Didn't just squash him," Stone said as he swung his feet around on the bed and set them down on the rug-covered floor. "Cut him to ribbons and left him for the vultures, the centipedes, and the worms. Wouldn't even kill him, the bastards. He'd been lying out there for days—alive. Just a piece of meat for the world to feast on."

"Well, I'm through here. That's for damn sure. I've had a long haul," the ancient whore said with a dark laugh. "And God knows, if the Lord above opened the narrow doors of heaven another ten miles, I still wouldn't be able to get inside. But I'll tell you as I stand before you, I've had enough. I ain't whoring and I ain't ice picking no more." She closed her eyes with an almost religious intensity, and Stone saw little rivulets of water seep out from each side of her eyes and trace little slick tracks through her thick makeup. They actually carved out the powder, digging down nearly an eighth of an inch into the stuff, so it looked as if little ditches were being dug down each side of her face.

"Well, I'm most proud to witness your conversion," Stone said as he set himself up on both legs and started wobbling immediately. "But really, what I want is to find April. Do you have any idea where she is, where they've taken her? Any of the other girls heard of a young, real pretty girl, they'd undoubtedly be marking her as a virgin—if they're selling her."

"Haven't heard a thing," Peaches said, drying her eyes with a perfumed handkerchief. The moment the excess moisture had been wiped up, she pulled a little makeup tin from her omnipresent purse and began dabbing at it, slamming the thick powder onto her cheeks, sending up a cloud of the stuff all around head so she half disappeared for a moment. "But you could try Main Square—it's the center of the mall—where the best, the most high-priced weapons and girls are. The Fifth Avenue, so to speak, of the place. If they're selling your sister as high-priced virgin meat, that's for sure where they'd stash her. That's the only advice I can give you, sweetie pie. But be careful. If there is a trap being set for someone here in Keenesburg, it can only be for you. If your sister is the bait, then they'll be waiting, Stone. Waiting to cut you down. You're luckier than a prairie mouse that fell into a rattlesnake den that you're even still alive. That dumb disguise of yours wouldn't have lasted another day here. Believe me. The lower-level assholes are just amoeba brains, but the upper echelons—the Scalzannis, his brothers, the dons, all of them—they're sharp as hawks. They see anything funny. They have their eyes on this place like you wouldn't believe. Even got video cameras on all the major mall corridors, sweeping back and forth in case anyone tries to break through the windows and take anything.

"I'll have to take my chances," Stone said, finding that as he walked around the floor of the Howard Johnson's circa 1960s decorated room with pinups of naked girls from old *Penthouse* and *Playboy* magazines glued onto the walls, his legs seemed to grow a little steadier. "She's my blood. All that's left of it. If I don't save her, she's dead meat." He didn't add that he also felt responsible for the death of his father and mother—and that if April was taken, too, it would have been a bases-loaded home run in the kill-your-own-family department. In which case he might as well join them. For the feelings that would have been created in him would have been unbearable.

"This way, then, Stone," she said, taking him by the elbow in the same ironlike grip she had exhibited on the barroom floor. She opened up the little door in the wall and started pulling on some of the ropes that dangled in front of her, like nooses ready to be flung around necks. "They'd notice you if you tried to go back down the stairs. It's slow back there tonight. They was all joking about how dumb you looked as they carried you up here." Stone leaned forward and looked down the long, dark shaftway. It seemed that he was trusting his life to strangers more and more these days.

"Well, if I have to, then I guess I have to," Stone said as he sat up on the ledge and wriggled his way in so that he was sitting on top of the little wooden box once used to take away garbage, that had risen up to the third floor of the building he was in.

"It's not that far—just goes down four stories to the basement. Get out there and go through the corpse room—shouldn't be too busy—then right out to the street. Good luck, Stone. You're sure as hell going to need it."

"Thanks again for the 'no ice pick' policy," Stone said with a half grin. Then he disappeared into the darkness. As he put his full weight on the top of the dumbwaiter, it suddenly started shooting down faster than he had expected. By the time he got his hands back around the thick, fraying ropes that held the thing, it had already fallen to the first floor. He grabbed hard with both hands and nearly screamed as the rope ripped across his skin, instantly burning it red on both palms. The wooden box came to a hard thump on the concrete floor of the basement, and Stone went flying out through the air into a bunch of tables and chairs.

Don't make noise, Stone thought to himself with a bitter mental laugh as he rolled to a stop amid a deafening clatter of tables and chairs that were flying every which way. He rose to his feet, whipping out his Uzi, which he threw onto full auto and gripped hard around the frame-only magna stock. He was in a long and fairly narrow room with concrete block walls and a single dangling light bulb lighting the entire basement chamber, which was about eighty by ten feet. The tables he had knocked over lay mixed with a half dozen chairs, and Stone saw two corpses by the flickering light—both with purple faces and severed spinal cords waiting for the pit. He waited motionless, ready to kill, but no one showed up for the party. After about thirty seconds he let out a deep sigh and realized he hadn't breathed since he'd hit the floor. He was luckier than his ass deserved. Whoever was supposed to be around here wasn't anywhere in sight—or hearing distance. Off somewhere fucking or getting stoned. Thank God for drugs and women, Stone thought as he started forward through a dark, narrow passageway. They had just saved his ass.

It was easy to get outside, as Stone didn't find a single guard in the lower level. He came to a ramp and then was out on a side street. He walked without the cap or glasses now but pulled the leather collar of his thickly lined field jacket up around his neck to hide at least part of his lower face. It was late now, even for the mall—four-thirty in the morning—and Stone only encountered stragglers here and there, staggering back to their rooms with whores under each arm, bottles in each hand.

He made his way toward the center of the mall as Peaches had suggested, keeping a wary eye out for the surveillance cameras that he saw posted here and there at major intersections of the larger corridors. Stone just had to pray that the scumbag at the controls of the thing was asleep at the wheel, as most of these goons were. Then he came to what was obviously the main thoroughfare. Here, the store windows were all gilded in fake gold, with real glass nearly an inch thick that rose up high, framing its contents. Stone walked slowly along, looking deeply in each window. It was the crème de la crème of rifles in the first few stores. Handcrafted and carved, with finished walnut stocks and stainless-steel parts. These were the collector's editions—available only to the top warlords, the deacons in the church of crime.

After several blocks the windows were filled with girls again. But these weren't whores, used up and scarred like a canyon. These were young, rosy-faced teens and young women just captured from the Styx, from wagon parties, from raiders, from all over the region. The most desirable of the young beauties that were for sale in the mall. The ones that the richest of the death dealers were after. The guns they bought, but it was the girls,—the sweet, young, angelic virgins—they craved, that they bid against each other for, that they drove by cars and armored vehicles a thousand miles to visit the slave stores of the Scalzanni Mall. Quality was quality, and though Scalzanni was one of the biggest sons of a bitches in the West, he delivered. His reputation for carrying untouched, unblemished meat was unmatched.

Even now, in the dying hours of the night, Stone saw a pining figure here and there staring at some lovely thing who lay fast asleep in the window, looking at her with wild, lusting eyes. Dreaming, dreaming. None of them paid Stone the slightest notice as he walked by. Each of the girls was back-

dropped by some mythical scene or other to add fantasy to
the crude reality of being imprisoned in a glass cage but a
few feet wide, naked for thousands of drooling men to see.
Behind one girl were crude paintings of ancient Egypt. She
had a necklace around her neck, attempting to approximate
the Cleopatra look. Another display had a Revolutionary
War motif with George Washington crossing the Delaware.
Its nude sixteen-year-old occupant wore only an American
flag around her groin, held there by but a single ready-to-
snap thread. Yet another naked teen appeared to be in the
deep woods with a little leaf glued over each breast.

And so it went as Stone walked slowly down the length
of the main corridor, where the "expensive goods" lay,
glancing back and forth from side to side as he passed each
absurd display. He had nearly reached the very end when he
glanced ahead at a single cage that stood by itself, marking
the very end of the long walkway. The glass cage was larger,
the lighting brighter on this one than on any of the others.
And as Stone drew closer he could see that the scene painted
on the back of the cage was a mock Renaissance one—with
storm clouds all around and angels flying down. And the
girl—chained naked to a tree in this tableau—was his sister.

Stone rushed forward, knowing he was losing his cool.
But he couldn't stand seeing her tied up like an animal, her
uncovered nakedness but for a small crown she wore on her
head as if she were some medieval princess. He came right
up to the glass covering and pressed his face against it. She
was so close—right on the other side—yet as if in another
dimension. Her eyes were closed tight, and Stone could see
by her slow breathing and sallow complexion that they had
drugged her. He hit against the side of the glass with his fist,
then harder, trying to wake her. Before he knew what he was
doing, he was pounding against the glass with both fists in a
fury of rage and murderous intent against the bastards who
had done this.

Suddenly her eyes seemed to tremble slightly, and they
opened just a hair. The pupils within seemed to focus on
Stone, and suddenly the eyes opened almost halfway.

"Martin . . ." The lips formed silently, hardly moving. "Martin . . ." Then she seemed to fall back into a swoon, her head dropping back to the side. Stone was beside himself with rage, wanting to reach her. He reached down and pulled out his Ruger .44 Mag and stepped back. He knew somewhere inside himself that he probably shouldn't be doing this, that as Peaches had said, they'd be watching him. But he also knew that direct action is the only way to make things happen. And that you could sit around for a million years and wonder about the consequences of things—or just do them.

Stone was for doing something now—and getting the hell out of there with her. Maybe it wouldn't be that hard. Maybe. He aimed the .44 at the very side of the glass where the two edges met, as far away from April as he could. Turning his own head and shielding it with his other hand, Stone fired. Without looking to see what damage he had wrought, he raised the gun up a foot, fired again, then up another foot or so for a final blast. He turned and saw that it had worked—at least partially. The thick glass had shattered for yards in each direction but still hung together by invisible shatterproof threads within. Stone reached forward and punched at it, making a hole so that he could reach inside and pull whole sections of the broken window out.

Within thirty seconds Stone had cleared out a space big enough to crawl through and scrambled inside. He jumped up and rushed to April, who seemed to have fallen sound asleep again, even through the gun blasts. Stone pulled his Randall bowie knife from its sheath at his side and reached out to cut the leather thongs that held her upright, tied to two posts. Before he had even reached the first, there was a sudden hiss, and a yellow mist began pouring down from vents in the ceiling.

"Shit," Stone screamed as he ripped up the Ruger and fired three quick shots into the ceiling. But he knew even as he did so that it was a futile gesture. He couldn't shoot gas out of the fucking air—or even hit those who controlled it. It was only the pipes that released the quick-stun muscle gas so that it filled the glass box within seconds. Stone felt his mind sinking again down into a field of pain, as if he was being buried under the dirt by a plowed blanket of asphyxiating mud. The dirty air seemed to fill his lungs and his mouth. And then he was just a chunk of dirt himself, shouting but not being heard from beneath the falling earth of his mind.

Chapter Seventeen _____

Stone wondered if he was heading toward heaven or hell as he seemed to shoot down a long white tube of light that was all around him as if he was a moth caught inside a flourescent tube. He'd been basically a good fellow—relatively speaking, that was. Of course, he'd killed a number of men, but that had been since he left the bunker, and only when they tried to do him in first. Yes, all things considered, he certainly was a candidate for cloudland. On the other hand, he had no illusions about the entrance requirements. And though there was some good mixed in there in a few spots, realistically he was heading downstairs, a concept that, even though he was dead, didn't make him feel too good. Made his stomach crawl, in fact. Which made him wonder even as he shot faster through the tunnel of pure whiteness how dead men and souls could have stomachs.

Then he was rocketing toward the end, which grew brighter and brighter, and suddenly he was in a sea of colors and voices that blinded and deafened him instantly.

"He's coming around, he's coming around," a godlike creature seemed to bellow, and Stone's brainpan shook around like the bells at Notre Dame. "The asshole is coming to."

"Ah, how pleasant," a second voice thundering in over the first. "And I was just thinking I was going to have to leave without having any entertainment today. Mr. Stone, welcome to hell."

Stone slowly opened his eyes a painful fraction of an inch at a time. So it was hell—he'd been demoted. Ah, well. He tried to focus on the denizens of the subterranean world with a morbid curiosity as to just what the devil and his minions actually looked like. But the face that sprang into view as he squinted in the light of numerous fluorescent lights overhead was worse than what he had expected: Scalzanni cracking his knuckles and looking most pleased. The pointed rat face grinned down at Stone, who realized as his consciousness slowly began seeping back into his battered brain that not only was he not in hell, but that he was still alive and tied down flat on his back, hardly able to move an inch.

"My sister—" Stone began, suddenly remembering that she had been with him in his last seconds.

"Cool out, Stone," the Mafia crime boss said with a razor-sharp grin. He walked around the hospital bed, stripped of everything so that just a wide board was anchored to the frame, atop which Martin Stone lay naked, his hands and feet tied with unbreakable cords. "She's okay. Not that it's any of your fucking concern. She'll be marketed as one of my stable of virgins. She *is*, I hope." He sneered at Stone. "Or were you renting her out yourself, and that's why you came to get her back?" Scalzanni laughed a wet, little slurping sound, and his black silk suit danced around him as if it were far too big for the emaciated body that was hidden beneath it.

"Pig," Stone spat back, "you'd sell your own fucking mother for a nickel."

"Oh, it would take far more than a nickel to buy my mother." Scalzanni smirked. "Though to tell you the truth, there hasn't been a hell of a lot of demand for her lately— since she died." The Mafia crime lord laughed loud, and his two personal bodyguards, both looking like relatives of Bigfoot, laughed along with him, resulting in lots of snorting and general merriment. Stone took the few seconds to raise his head and see just where he was. He could only move his neck an inch or two by straining hard, and even then he had to lower his eyeballs until they were ready to slide out of their sockets to see anything. But from what he could vaguely discern, he was in a cinder-block room about forty feet long, fifteen or so wide. There were other men tied to beds and boards, all with contraptions covering some part of their body. Stone could hear low groans, an occasional loud one above the harsh laughs of the Mafia crew. The light from rows of fluorescent tubes above was blindingly intense. Whatever sick scenes were going on in this room of death, the management apparently wanted to be able to witness them in vivid, blazing Technicolor.

"Oh, I am a funny man," Scalzanni said at last, drying his eyes with a monogrammed purple handkerchief that he extracted from the pocket of his silk jacket. "Now tell me, Mr. Stone," Scalzanni said as he walked back into view above Stone's head. "What kind of pain would you like to feel today? We have so many 'styles' to choose from down here that sometimes I get lost myself."

"My sister," Stone began again, his brain chugging like a computer as he tried to think of anything he could use to bargain with the slime. "She's done nothing to you. Why don't you—"

"Ah, but I am letting her go," Scalzanni said, weaving his fingers together and snapping his knuckles, a habit Stone was rapidly growing to hate. "You're the one I want. Her—I'd rather make the bucks off selling her ass. She's going to get a good dollar, you goddamn better believe that. I've already had offers over $10,000 from some of the boys out West. She may bring in a record amount for a bitch."

Stone glared at the concave-faced weasel and was so filled with the desire to kill him that he couldn't even utter a word, just grow red in the cheeks and bite his teeth so they sounded like rocks grinding against one another.

"You shouldn't have killed my brother," Scalzanni said, the obscene smile suddenly vanishing from his face, taking on its normal undertaker look of imminent death. "Not that I liked the bastard," Scalzanni went on. "He tried to take me out once. Can you believe it—me, his own brother? Of course, I had tried to have him assassinated myself." He laughed but only for a second, then the face, which was nothing but yellow skin stretched as tight as a drum head over the protruding cheekbones beneath, grew as cold as the breath of winter itself.

"But we can try to kill each other—we're family. You can't. See, I gotta kill you, Stone, for honor's sake, for the respect of all the other crime clans. Otherwise they'd say Joey "Cheap" Scalzanni let this scumbag take out his own brother and didn't even do a thing about it. Not that I mind killing you, of course. In fact, I'm sure I'll enjoy it tremendously."

"I'm so glad to bring joy to a walking pile of vomit like you, Scalzanni. Now I know where my whole life has been leading all these years. My purpose on this earth."

"Goddamn right." the Mafia chief chortled back in that whispering kind of squeal that Stone found most disquieting. "Now, as I was saying," he went on as he walked out of his prisoner's view and over to some crates along one wall, "we get so much stuff going through here"—the warlord chuckled from across the room—"for selling, putting on display. But all the torture equipment—they pull it out for me so's I can see it first. Ain't they a great bunch of guys I got working for me?" Stone could hear him throwing metal things around, so they clanked against one another. "Ah, here it is—I been waiting for a set of these for months now."

He walked back into view, dangling two strange-looking little metal boxes with all kinds of levers and gears on them. "You know, there's so many ways to create pain in a man . . . or woman—there I go being sexist again." Scalzanni laughed. "All my whores tell me to watch out for that. But the feet—the feet, Stone," Scalzanni said excitedly, as if he were teaching Stone some great lesson that he would gratefully carry forward into life. "The feet are capable of the greatest fucking pain that a man can know."

"Is that so?" Stone asked with a bored expression as he tried to wriggle his toes. His feet had been doubly bound at each corner of the bed so that his exposed soles extended over the board. He couldn't move them an inch. Suddenly he felt hands on them, and then cold metal against the tops and bottoms of each foot. Then something much worse. Needles or nails—hundreds of them—pressing against every square inch of each of the soles. They were sharp, pointed like sewing needles, and even just resting against his skin, but not breaking, it caused waves of pain to shoot up and down his legs.

"You see, the feet have the most nerve endings in the entire body," Scalzanni went on from the foot of the bed. "Did you know that, Stone? Isn't that something? The goddamn soles of the feet have the most fucking nerve endings per cubic whatever-the-fuck-it-is of any part of the human anatomy. To demonstrate, let me just tighten this lever here." The Mafia chief began turning some little wheel on the side of one of the metal boxes, and the needles began moving forward a thousandth of an inch at a time. Stone felt some of them pop through the skin and winced hard as his whole body tried to arch up on the board. It did hurt—like a motherfucker.

"There, isn't that an interesting sensation?" Scalzanni asked, coming into view again so the pointed face was staring down at him. "And you know what? The deeper I push them needles, the more it hurts. Ain't that something?" He smiled at Stone, the iron smile of the cold killer. "So you and me gonna have a lot of fun. Keep it going for days. But first I got a meeting I can't miss. Biggest sale ever of firepower to the West Coast Guardians of Hell. Make me the biggest son of a bitch in this whole area." He disappeared again, and Stone felt the needles on the second torture shoe being pushed in a little farther. Both legs now were filled with the paralyzing rushes of pure pain. "Otherwise I wouldn't dream of straying from this little party," Scalzanni said. "But don't worry—I'll be back. Real soon. So you just think about how this feels and know that it's going to get a lot worse. A whole lot worse." The Mafia don giggled again, and then Stone heard feet stomping and a door open and close.

He tried to move his mind away from the pain. Tried every mind trick he could remember his father telling him about to avoid the sensation of pain. Drop your center, breathe deep, go into your mind. . . . All good advice, but like all good advice, a million times easier said than carried out. Especially when his feet felt like pincushions. He heard footsteps walking fully around the room as if checking on all its victims, and then a door opening again and closing.

They were alone. The assholes had left them unguarded. Somehow Stone fought against the searing pain from his feet and again raised his head up. He was bound down so securely that it placed a terrific strain on his neck and shoulder muscles to raise up, but he did, welcoming the new pain as a relief from the blistering soles of his feet.

There were five others in the cinder-block room. Each of them in some torture device of his own. The man immediately to Stone's left—his whole head was inside of a metal mask, nothing else on his body touched. Beyond him, Stone could see just a head poking free from the top of a coffinlike box that contained him from thighs to neck. His eyes were open, but he stared straight ahead as if unseeing. Far down the room, Stone could see what looked like a steel vat perhaps eight feet wide and six feet high. A man hung suspended above it from ropes on a pulley that were fitted around his shoulders. He had been lowered into the vat to the waist, but other than that he didn't look as if they had tried to slice him or anything. His eyes, too, were open, staring off somewhere into a private hell that was uncommunicable.

"Anyone alive out there?" Stone said, though the use of his mouth just made the pain burn out down at his feet. "Any of you poor bastards alive?"

"I—I am, I think," the man to the left of Stone whispered back, though it was hard to hear him clearly through the iron mask.

"What . . . what have they done to you?" Stone asked as he tried to keep his mind on his words and the other poor son of a bitch, and away from the puncturing needles that were ripping into his own nerve endings.

"My face—they've put spikes through it. Slowly they keep moving deeper into me. I—I—"

"And I—" another voice hissed out from the coffinlike structure past the masked man. "They've put me in this damn iron maiden." Stone could just see the head poking from the top of the thing like a mummy who hadn't been completely sealed in. "God, it hurts. I think the spikes have pierced my organs now. There are hundreds of them—hundreds—"

"Me—" another voice croaked out through the blood scented-air. "They've stripped all my skin off of me—sliced it with scalpels. I have no flesh from my neck down. Oh, God—I can feel my muscles and veins twitching in the cold air. Kill me—someone kill me. I beg you."

"And him," Stone asked as he caught the eye of the head that stared at him from the top of the spiked coffin. "The one in the swimming pool—what's his brand of torture?"

"Him," the head said with a grim smile that Stone thought quite admirable considering the fact that the wretched bastard was being pierced clear through by a hundred barbecue skewers, "he's floating in acid, man. Pure sulfuric acid. There ain't a drop of him left below the water line."

Stone craned his neck as far as it would go and got another glimpse of the body suspended above the vat. To his horror, the eyes on the thing opened and gazed back at him with a pain beyond the pale. And suddenly, just having his own feet turned into porcupine parking lots didn't seem so bad—compared to a man whose legs, hips—and balls—had all been melted away. A man who was only half there.

Chapter Eighteen _____

S tone had been wrong when he woke up and thought he was still alive. He *was* in hell. Nothing could be more horrible than this. They broke off conversation—if the grunts and moans that were emitted from each torture implement were language—when the door suddenly flew open again and one of the guards made his rounds of the torturees to make sure they weren't trying anything funny. Though how any of them would quite go about such a thing in the condition they were in was not something he wondered about.

"Yo—acid man," the guard said as he came up to the vat of acid with the man dangling in it. "You still kicking or what?" He put his face real close to the tied-up victim to look into his unblinking eyes, though he found it hard to imagine that the sucker could still be alive. He had been lowered into the vat nearly forty-eight hours ago—inch by agonizing inch. First his toes and feet had been dissolved, then his calves. All the way to where it had reached now— about three inches above the hips, where it had dissolved his genitalia and lower organ tracts.

"I said 'yo, acid man,' are you still—" But he stopped in mid-sentence as the dangling half corpse suddenly opened its pale lips and spat at him, catching the gray jumpsuit-clad torture attendant right in the eye. The guard jumped back, as if he'd been stung with poison, and wiped at his eye furiously, apparently enraged and maddened by the transfer of human body mucus from that—"thing"—to him. The other prisoners—those who could see or make sounds, which was a grand total of three—all made attempts at cheering noises at the way the half-man had stood up to the guard.

"Scum, scum," the guard bellowed, retreating backward from the room to wash the death slime off his face. "You'll feel my anger when I return." He stormed out of the place, slamming the door so hard that the needles on Stone's feet shook and seemed to drive another fraction of an inch deeper. Just what the hell the asshole guard intended to "punish" them with was beyond Stone's, or any of the other torture victims', imaginations. Things were, to say the least, already in a fairly painful state for all of them.

Suddenly the Mafia guard was back, throwing the door open and standing at the entrance in a dramatic pose with some kind of barbed-wire whip in his hands, and he snapped it through the air so it made a whistling sound.

"Now, who was laughing?" the guard said, walking forward with loud, stomping steps so his boots echoed ominously within the cinder-block walls. "I said who was—" Suddenly Stone heard a rushing sound and a loud groan. He craned hs neck to see what the hell was happening and got a whiff of strong perfume. *Peaches!* The name shot through his mind just as his eyes caught the range of a bizarre sight. The whore had her hand around the guard's mouth and was pulling his whole head backward. At the same time she was driving her "ice pick" clean through the torture tech's neck. As she sort of steered the package of jerking meat forward, she continued to twist the steel blade back and forth, making sure every nerve was cut. When she was satisfied, the ancient hooker ripped the ganglia-cutter out and kicked the body forward hard, her big leg, varicose veins and all, swinging up from beneath her pink tafetta gown. The dead meat flew forward across the room, not stopping until its head smashed into the far wall, where it exploded in pieces and dribbled down the wall onto the quivering corpse that lay on the floor.

"Stone, Stone," Peaches exclaimed, slipping the long ice pick up her sleeve in an instant. She ran over to him, rolling around like a bathtub of Jell-O beneath her mountainous dress. "What the hell have they done to you?"

"I think I'm being fitted for shoes," Stone whispered through gritted teeth, as he didn't want her to see or hear the kind of pain he was in. "Said they'd gone to check if they had my size."

"Well, these are a little tight, my asshole friend. In fact," she said with a grunt as she found the release lever on both the torture implements, "I'd say they're making your feet bleed." She gingerly pulled first one, then the other, device out, so that the needles slipped carefully out of Stone's skin. They'd only penetrated about a quarter of an inch, but as Scalzanni had noted, the body had a shitload of nerves down there.

"Thanks," Stone said as she sliced through the leather thongs that bound him with a scalpel she picked up from a table filled with things that cut next to Stone's hospital bed. "I was writing my will in my head—not that I have anything to give anyone. Why did you come?" he asked as he swung his body around to the side of the board and carefully lowered his feet to the concrete floor.

"I told you, I had enough of this place. I heard the scuttle when I hit the streets this morning—that they caught someone. Someone big. I figured it would only be you. I heard of this place. Everyone has, but this is the first time I've actually paid it a visit." She shuddered as she looked around the room and saw the mind-boggling devices of pain that the others were in. "Good God, I—I—" Even the toughest old whore this side of the Chicago Stockyards was taken aback by the sheer horror of it all.

She walked over to the masked man and touched his shoulder gently. A groan was the only answer.

"I'm going to cut you free," the whore said, hefting the scalpel again and releasing the man from his bonds. "I don't know if you can move or what but it—" Before she could finish, the torture victim sat up and swung his legs over the side. Peaches almost puked when she saw the flood of blood sweep down out of the sides of the mask. She didn't want to know what was going on inside it.

Meanwhile Stone was putting his feet down on the

ground as carefully as if they were made of eggs. They hurt like the blazes. But not as much as they did a minute ago when the needles had still been in them. He stood up, and an involuntary scream escaped from his dry lips. As Peaches moved on to the next man like some garishly made-up angel of mercy, Stone saw her suddenly look over at him, about twelve feet away. He realized for the first time that he was stark naked and, in the midst of all the blood and death, unconsciously threw his hand over his pelvic region.

"If you think I come all this way," Peaches said with a laugh as she caught the motion out of her all-seeing eyes, "just to see your wang, you got another think coming." She kept talking to keep her spirits up as she walked toward the upright iron maiden, the head in it staring back at her with dim, pain-swollen eyes. " 'Cause, honey child, I seen more damn dicks in my time than there are trees in the Rocky Mountains. Seen 'em the size of pencils, seen 'em the size of baseball bats; seen white ones, and brown ones and purple ones; I seen straight ones and curved ones and broken ones; I seen . . ." She went on talking and cackling like an insane woman, but Stone could see, as he hobbled across the cold concrete floor, that she was helping the men. A few twitching smiles ran like currents across some of the other victims' faces.

Stone found his things on one of a row of shelves in which all their clothes and weapons had been placed—for later use or sale. He dressed as fast as he could, wincing again as he stepped into his boots. But he was so damn happy to still be alive—and have some firepower—that he pushed the pain down and told it to go fuck itself. By the time he stood up, Peaches had released four of them. They weren't in good shape by a long shot. Stone was amazed that they could even move. But there they were—the mask man, the coffin man, the one with nails driven into his head. Even the man who had been skinned alive was somehow sitting up, all his exposed musculature pulsing and rippling with slime.

Peaches started toward the one suspended over the acid vat and reached out for him. How she could reach through one's natural disgust at the states of these men was incredi-

ble to Stone. But then, she had been dealing with men all
her life. In her own way, perhaps she had always been an
angel to those she had served. She reached the hanging half-
man and pulled the wheel-mounted pulley system that held
him over the vat back so that he was completely free of it.
Even the others gasped—those who could still see, anyway.
He was a half-man. His intestines, everything within, showing within plain view. It was as if he had been sliced in half
by a guillotine and it was there for all the world to see. Only
the fact that the chemical burning action of the acid had sort
of sealed the whole bottom kept what was inside from falling
out onto the floor. Peaches held out a hand to stroke his
sweat-soaked forehead when the door swung open again,
and before a single one of them could move, another guard
rushed forward with .45 in hand.

He fired without saying a word, at the first person he saw
move in the torture room, which happened to be Peaches.
The slug slammed dead center in her forehead, drilling
through a wall of brain tissue and then out the back. She
stopped dead in her tracks, frozen like an ice sculpture, and
then toppled backward and flat onto her back, as dead as all
her relatives. The guard turned sharply, a wild look in his
eye as he saw the dead body of his compatriot on the floor.
But as he leaned forward and let the gun drop for a second, a
shape launched itself from the other side of the door. Stone,
who had hidden from the guard when he burst in, came at
the murderer from the right. As the man turned, trying to
level his pistol, Stone came into him with his shoulder like a
linebacker making a crunching block. The guard's .45 flew
into the air as he careened sideways across the floor. He
screamed as he saw what was coming but was unable to do a
goddamn thing to stop it. He hit the metal rim, and the
whole top part of his body flew over the side and into the
acid.

There was a terrific commotion with hands flying around
in the air and the burning liquid foaming like a boiling stew
on the top of the vat. But not for long. Within seconds the
guard was still, his waist draped over the side of the steel
vat, as if he were washing his face. Stone walked over to the
motionless body now that the waters had calmed down a

little. He gripped his hand around the lower back of the man's jacket and pulled. And what came out was not something even the devil dared dream about.

Stone let the faceless and handless thing fall to the floor as he walked over to Peaches. She was as dead as you can get, her eyes wide open, staring up at the ceiling, already drying out as her body began losing moisture, cooling and beginning to rot.

"You old whore," he whispered with tenderness in his voice, reaching down and closing the eyes with his hand so they didn't have to be extinguished by being exposed to such harsh light. "You're the bravest damn woman I've ever met." With that, he turned to see what was left.

Not much. The little group of should-be-dead men were gathered together waiting. Waiting for what, Stone couldn't imagine. Not one of them even should have been alive. He walked over to them, and those that could, stared back at him with barely opened eyes. One guy with his head in a spike-filled mask; one guy with his body in a coffin piercing him from neck to groin; one guy with nails hammered into his head so he looks like a bloody ice-cream cone with three-penny sprinkles; one guy with all his skin peeled off so he looked like an overgrown, peeled grape; and one guy with only the top of him left, and all his guts ready to spill out over the floor like a broken garbage bag. Just the kind of crowd Stone loved to hang out with.

"All right," he said suddenly, taking charge. Whatever they looked like, however long they had left on this earth, Stone had to get them and his own ass out of there—and fast. Scalzanni could be back at any minute—or a contingent of guards. "We're getting the hell out of here, right now. You!" he said, grabbing at the sleeve of the nail-headed fellow. The man's eyes swiveled around like a cow's, as empty and dumb as the dirt beneath its feet. But he let Stone lead him over to the half-man, who hung as if in a swing from the mobile pulley system.

"You push," Stone said to the huge fellow, who seemed to have lost just about everything that had once been stored inside the brain. Still, he allowed his hands to be guided to the sidebars of the pulley and nodded once with a spit-dribbling smile, as if indicating that he knew what was expected.

"You!" Stone said, pointing to the coffin man, who, with his legs outside the knitting-needle-filled box, was apparently able to walk, albeit in tremendous pain. He looked almost comical, like a turtle with a huge wooden shell on its back. But Stone didn't laugh. "Lead him." He reached out and placed the right hand of the marked victim on the coffin man's shoulder.

Stone turned and asked the skinless man, "Can you move?" To Stone he was the worst of the lot, even more horrific than the half-man. But he made himself look fully into the torture victim's pain-shattered eyes. Only mucus, red and wet, and veins and tendons that seemed to undulate like a million little worms over his body covered him now. The face, too—carved down to the muscles of the cheeks, the tendons that operated the jaws and mouth long and leathery. Yet amazingly it could talk.

"Lead on, Moses," the bloody lips intoned hoarsely. "Deliver me to the Promised Land." It laughed, and the motion made stuff fall off its face and arms, a pulsing gelatinlike substance that sprinkled onto the floor.

"Okay, fellow torturees, let's get the fuck out of here," Stone said as he started carefully toward the door, his Uzi in his hand, ready to spray out a wall of death. He moved carefully through the door, surveying the darkened hallway that led off it. He walked down the hall in slow, peculiar steps, as his feet still felt like his socks were made of glass. He could feel the blood that continued to ooze out from the myriad little holes in the soles of his feet, making his boots produce an obscene sucking sound.

Behind him it was the brainless leading the blind, leading the ugly, or something like that. The bizarre crew made its way down the flat cement corridor. They pulled and pushed and wheeled one another down the hall, making all kinds of wet sounds mixed in with the continued groans and little squeals of pain that emitted from one or another of them every few seconds—as their own personal pain device dug a little deeper into them from the motion.

Stone moved about twenty feet ahead as they came to a

larger hall that from the sudden draft of air he knew must lead out. He had barely taken two steps down it when he felt something land around his neck, and before he knew what was happening, he was being pulled backward off-balance. By the sharp pain that dug into his throat Stone knew instantly what it was—a garrote. He and his father had practiced with the damn little loops of wire enough times for him to know what the hell they were. And he had been suckered into one. He also knew that there was no return once they got you firmly noosed—that he would be dead in another ten seconds. The wire bit into Stone's throat like a loop of fire, and he saw everything bursting with explosions of red all around him as his eyes nearly popped out of his skull.

Suddenly the wire loosened and he was gasping for breath. He turned as consciousness flowed back into his blood-starved brain and raised his Uzi, which was still in his hand. But there was no need. The others were already upon the guard. The multilated men were all around him, pulling him back and down, their bloody hands reaching out and clawing at him. When they stepped back a minute later, there wasn't a hell of a lot left of the bastard.

"Come on," Stone said hoarsely when he at last had regained his breath. He edged forward again, this time his eyes darting back and forth like a lizard's, as he sure as hell wasn't about to allow himself to be jumped a second time. But the way was clear along the basement corridor, and within a couple of minutes they reached a ramp that led up and into an open space. Stone searched around at the top of the ramp, but though there was a chair leaned back against the wall, no guard was in sight.

"We're out," Stone said as he motioned for them to come up the ramp. Pushing each other, grunting and breathing like dying men, they somehow hobbled up the incline after him. Stone unlatched a steel gate and let them file past in their mobile freak parade before he closed it again. No sense in letting the bastards know in which direction the escapees had gone. They hightailed it—or as fast as a crew of the walking falling-apart can go—into the shielding woods. Stone led them into the increasingly thick pockets of trees for about ten minutes, until they were at least momentarily safe.

"Well," Stone started to say to the ragged, bloody crew with their masks and nails and flesh dripping off and what all, but the half-man, of all people, spoke up as he dangled from the pulley cart, the blank-faced nail head still pushing from behind.

"You don't have to say anything," the half-man croaked out, hardly moving its lips at all, its eyes only open as wide as razor slits. "There is nothing to say. We're all dead men. But at least we'll die free—and not in that stinking room. Thank you."

"Thank you, thank you," mumbled the others who could still talk. Even the soon-to-die wanted to go out on their own terms.

"Now go," the half-man commanded Stone as he pointed to push him deeper into the comforting woods. "Go, for you are still of the world of the living. We are not!" Stone knew that it was true. There wasn't a man among them who would see the next moonrise. He had done what he could—as little as it was.

"Then God—God help you," Stone said softly. He stood and watched silently for about half a minute as they lurched and crawled and led each other deeper into the dark woods, which stood cold but loving, ready to take them all into its earthen bed.

Chapter Nineteen _____

S tone tore ass through the woods that ran along the perimeter of the mall for nearly half a mile. He kept about twenty feet inside the shielding trees, but he could see the outer edge of the sick shopping mart, and down its corridors where contented killers strolled, examining this Pandora's box filled with the appliances of murder. Stone kept his Ruger .44 in one hand as he ran—just in case. The heavy load it carried would do just fine to slam right through small branches and brush—and into an attacker's skull. He had just about reached the end of the mall when he heard bells going off at the far end—where he had just escaped from. They knew. The shit was hitting the fan. He just didn't want to get sprayed.

When he reached the end of the mall, Stone stayed in the woods until he was yet another quarter of a mile or so past it. Whatever their security apparatus, he could see, it wasn't super-efficient, as he saw not a guard in sight. Making sure there was no posse, Stone edged toward the line of trees and then dashed out into the open, beelining along a wide dirt road toward the garage where the Harley and his dog sat waiting. He had sort of lost track of time, of how long he had been gone. It seemed like only hours, yet somewhere he must have lost a night or a day. Something was wrong. If he lived through the next few hours, he'd get it all straightened out.

Stone's feet hurt like he was doing long-distance running

on razor blades. On one particularly sharp stab of pain, he threw his head back and winced, noticing that the sky was looking bad. All the shit and poison that had been accumulating up there for days now was spinning and twisting around like blood inside a washing machine. The dark cloud cover had dropped so low, it seemed that he could almost jump up and touch it. The storm clouds were huge whales of things, brown- and purple-tinged, positively puffed out of every dark edge as if they couldn't contain the load in their radioactive guts much longer. And when they puked it all out, the world below would be in big trouble.

The prospect of being rained on by the radioactive showers was motivation enough for Stone. He took off even faster down the road, telling his goddamn screaming feet to just shut up or he'd shoot them off. At last the broken-down garage came into view, and Stone saw that Pliers actually had been doing some work. The bails of barbed wire he had had stored away had all been unraveled, and he had formed a barrier of the sharp stuff about five feet high and a yard wide that ran the perimeter of the place, nearly a hundred feet on a side.

"Hey, old man," Stone yelled out, cupping his hands together as he reached what had been the access road, which was now protected by the wall of dagger-tipped wire. "Hey, Pliers," Stone yelled out again, starting to get a little nervous, holding his .44 up to chest level, trying to sort things out in the dark. "Hey, I come for my dog and my—"

"Hold your damn horses," a voice yelled out from the darkness. Suddenly Stone saw a thin, flickering flame emerge from the little slabbed wood hovel the man lived in, and start to come toward him at a snail's pace in the dark. "You young folks want to do everything now—this instant. Can't wait a damn second. Why, when I—"

"Hurry up, old man," Stone yelled out impatiently, "or you'll have the whole damn Mafia army breathing down your throat. You don't want to get caught with me here, pal, so move it." The possibility of violence being done to hs little home made the old tinkerer move faster, and the sliver of candle flame bent almost sideways as he pushed through the night.

"Here," he said as he came up to Stone just on the other side of the barbed-wire wall. "I put this damn stuff up. Now I feel imprisoned in my own damn home." The old man laughed with a bitter snort as he undid some wires around a pole, and lifting one six-foot section of the barbed wire by a protected handhold, he pulled the whole piece back so Stone could slip through.

"Keep it open," Stone said as he came in on wobbly feet. "I'm out of here as soon as I get my bike going."

"What—what happened?" the old man asked nervously as he glanced back down the dark dirt road searching for signs of life. But he saw nothing—so far.

"Look, pal, I didn't tell you because it was none of your business—and because if you knew, if they found you, they would've tortured you until—ah, you don't even want to know. Anyway, I'm Martin Stone. Enemy number-one on their most-wanted list—bring in dead only."

"Well, I don't care what you done," Pliers said as he walked along beside Stone, who was headed over toward the barn where his Harley sat hidden. "Any enemy of those scum, as far as I'm concerned, is a friend of mine. But you better head out along the back roads. They'll send out super-souped-up cars on the main road—catch anything that moves. I'll show you the way."

"Ain't going that way," Stone said as he nearly stumbled, making his way over some loose boards just inside the barn. "My sister's back there—I'm going in for her."

"You'll n-never make it," Pliers said, stuttering in sheer terror at the thought as he tried to light the way ahead, his hand held out to the side and grasping the flickering candle. "Those guys are—I mean, I've seen them—I mean—"

"Skip it, old man," Stone said as he saw the black Harley sitting there like a bull in the gray-streaked darkness. "Where's the damn dog?" Stone said, looking around.

"Where is that little—" Pliers asked with a tone of incredible weariness in his voice. "From the moment you left, that son of a bitch was nothing but a ball of trouble. Got into every damn thing in the place—opened up every crate, pulled out every supply. And when it comes to eating, damn thing slurped up the first helping I gave before I even put it down. Lucky to get my hand out in one piece. And then it looks up at me and growls. Like there'd better be more or— Little mutt scared me, I'll tell you. So I just kept feeding him and feeding him every time I came out near the barn. Or else the growls would start up from the darkness. Why, that mutt of yours gobbled down in two days what my own damn dog eats in about a month. What's wrong with the creature —thyroid trouble, worms?"

"The only trouble with that dog is his fucking brains are screwed on backward," Stone said, whistling loudly into the darkness. "He thinks the entire planet and everybody on it are here for one purpose—to serve him. He thinks he's a king—when he's just a stinkin' dog. You hear that," Stone bellowed into the spiderwebbed rafters of the dusty barn. "You're just a fucking dog—now get out here. 'Cause I'm starting this bike up and moving out. And when the Mafia gets here and finds Martin Stone's dog, I think they're going to be very pleased about that."

As if getting the drift, if not the grammatical subtleties, of Stone's words, a low shape came lumbering out from a corner of the place, its long, untrimmed nails plopping down with lazy steps. "Well, his highness makes an appearance," Stone said with biting sarcasm. "You look like shit—you know that, dog?" Stone said, shaking his head as he saw the apparition that suddenly staggered into view and stood next to the Harley, lit up by the now straight candle flame. The animal was covered with dust—and food. The old man had apparently fed the pitbull so much out of his fearful state that pieces of meat, bread, and milk, actually covered the animals' head and back. Its stomach was so distended, Stone swore it would drag an ant's back walking along the ground.

"Get on," Stone said with disgust. "Either I'm sending you to finishing school—or off to live with the goddamn cannibals. The way they eat, you'd be right at home there." Stone started the motor of the Harley, and the pitbull let out a little whine as it looked up at the seat that, from its vantage point, looked about a mile high. But as its master started slowly easing the bike forward, the pitbull let out a quick bark and leapt up. Usually it would have been no problem. The pitbull had made the jump from the ground to the back of the seat hundreds of times. But with the additional ten or fifteen pounds it had deposited away, its trajectory sort of petered out before it really got going. It got its front paws on the back but not its rear ones, and hobbled along on its back legs like some sort of circus animal behind Stone's motorcycle.

"Good God," Stone exclaimed as he glanced around and saw the ridiculous dancing dog coming up behind. He stopped the bike, letting the animal catch up and somehow drag itself up, like a turtle up the side of Mt. Everest. "Try to leave the place with a little style, a little cool," Stone muttered to the animal, and it snorted back at him as if nothing untoward had happened, though it couldn't look him in the eye and settled down quickly on the leather seat ready for some heavy-duty digestive sleep.

Stone started the Electraglide forward, his eyes having adjusted to the darkness enough to see well now.

"More money—for the food, for your damn dog," Pliers demanded, shuffling through the creaking darkness alongside Stone's bike as they headed toward the front barn door.

"Forget it, pal," Stone snapped back. "I gave you a small fortune already and you know it. Thanks for the service. And I apologize for any discourtesy and bluffed biting this mutt may have inflicted on you. And one final bit of advice," Stone said as he reached the outside air.

"What the hell is that?" Pliers yelled out through the darkness now that his candle had blown out from a puff of night wind.

"If those sons of bitches show up here, don't let on you ever knew, saw, or talked to me—or my dog. Or you're a dead man." With that Stone accelerated slightly and eased through the narrow opening of the barbed wire. He slid back down the road, almost not moving for about fifty yards, high light off, the engine on a super-muffled low purr in neutral. He edged the bike along, kicking it with his legs until the saw a small path almost hidden by the bushes off to one side. Stone steered the bike onto it and saw within a few yards that it was an old path, probably used by cattle or deer decades ago but tamped down enough for him to make his way bent over through the bushes, which reached out from every side with twigs and thorns like a gauntlet of a million stabbing arms.

The dog didn't like it. Unprotected by thick outerwear like Stone, it got scraped all over its hide by all kinds of scratching tendrils. It kept letting out little yelps of pain and disturbed whines for Stone's benefit up front. Which was all just fine with Martin Stone. The dog deserved a little penance, a little punishment for being such an asshole.

The mall came into view alongside them, though dimly, about a hundred yards off through the trees. But he could see the lights from the displays, the lamps that stood on the corners flickering through the maze of branches that stood between him and the shopping center for all your murder needs. He gauged his approximate location by remembering certain signs he had seen when walking around the place and made a wide, circular route so he came out on the far side of the mall, past where he had made his escape from the torture room.

He slowed the bike down as the path suddenly opened up into a flat field of dirt, and Stone could see, as he let the Harley coast slowly forward, his fingers on the trigger of the .50-caliber machine gun that was mounted at the front of the motorcycle—that there was water, or liquid of some kind, ahead. He crossed the hundred yards or so of packed dirt, and his eyes squinted in the gray fog as he tried to make out what the shapes were that he saw sticking up here and there in the inklike water. The smell as he drew closer was sickening, a thick, meaty stench that filled the nostrils and lungs like a noxious gas.

Then all of a sudden he saw—and wished he hadn't—arms and legs floating everywhere. Head and feet and sex organs. There were parts of men and women bobbing around in a mini-sea of blackness. Stone brought the bike until it was about twenty feet from the edge and looked in. He could see fairly well, as the light from the mall itself drifted over and back, bouncing off trees and clouds even though they were several hundred yards away. Stone couldn't even see the other side of the lake, though he knew it had one. It was just that in the fog and mist that hovered over the place it seemed to disappear. Pieces of humanity were everywhere.

It was like an old auto junkyard, a swamp where the parts of useless vehicles were driven, thrown, buried. Only these were human vehicles. They had been used for their value to Scalzanni, and then turned into hulks, dismembered and thrown into this watery hell.

As he looked, Stone saw a snake slithering across the oily surface with a human hand in its jaws, taking it off to a more solid spot where it could be digested in peace. Stone turned as he heard a loud burp behind him and saw the dog staring toward the ocean of amputations too. It didn't look good. The pitbull's face seemed to turn green, and he jumped off the Harley suddenly, walked a few feet, and began puking.

"Oh, God," Stone said as he dismounted, throwing his hands up at the sky, which now rumbled with ominous thunder deep in the black guts of the mountainous clouds above. "What next, that's all I want to know," Stone mumbled half insanely. "What next?"

"Me, that's what's next," a voice, followed by a hellish cackle of laughter, came from off in the darkness. Stone's eyes rocketed over to the three figures approaching him— one small, two much larger on each side. The ratlike face came into view at about twenty yards away.

"Scalzanni," Stone spat out as he looked at the Mafia chieftain, still clad in his omnipresent black silk double-breasted suit.

"You were expecting the pope?" Scalzanni laughed, and the two psychos on each side of him emitted grunting noises that Stone took to be the same sort of general idea. "I don't know how you got out of that room, Stone, but no mind now. "I still got your sister. She's locked up right in that same cage you tried to heist her from. You want her, you come through me to get her." The Mafia top man reached inside his coat with a crossdraw as both arms formed an X for a second. When they came out, his hands were gripping the long, glistening, pointed meat hooks that Stone had hoped he wouldn't see again for a long, long time.

Stone reached for his .44 Redhawk, but both of the torpedoes already had rods in their hands and whipped them up so they were targeted on Stone's chest.

"Oh, that wouldn't be fair," Scalzanni commented as he

walked slowly toward Stone, twirling the flesh-rippers in each hand. "You and I—we're gong to have this out like men. Hand-to-hand. They'll make sure we stick to the rules."

"Rules—right." Stone smirked as he pulled his hand slowly away from his Magnum. "Well, can I use my damn knife?" he asked as the Mafia killer stalked closer. Stone opened his jacket slowly to show the bowie hanging there. He could hear the dog still puking its guts out about ten feet behind him on the other side of the Harley. Probably didn't even know that his master was about to become Italian cuisine.

"But of course," Scalzanni replied, motioning with his hooks for Stone to take it out. "The whole reason I ain't just shooting you dead right now is 'cause you got a big rep, asshole. Killing you would give me bragging rights all around these parts. So take out whatever toothpick you got in there, 'cause it ain't gonna do you a fucking bit of good." Stone took up the offer and slowly extracted the blade from his side, getting a good grip on it. He didn't really trust the torpedoes not to do him in. But they'd wait—until the last second. If their boss was winning, no guns. But if he started losing, Stone knew he'd have to be able to take out both of them too. Great.

He stepped away from the Harley and glanced down quickly at the ground around him, searching the dirt for any drops or obstructions, so he wouldn't get tangled up. He brought his eyes back up to the advancing Mafia killer. He'd seen the man do his thing with those hooks, and Stone had no illusions about the task ahead of him. The guy was small, as skinny as a fucking rail. But he was lethal with meat hooks. He circled slowly, planting one foot carefully down, then the next, making sure he made no mistakes.

"Don't be so shy," Scalzanni said, coming almost straight toward Stone now. "Got some friends who want to meet you." He held the hooks stretched out far at each end of his arm in the strange posture that Stone had seen him use just before he had killed the mountain man back at The Hot Load. Stone stepped back, not letting the arms get anywhere within reach.

This was the right thing to do. Scalzanni suddenly struck, swooping both hands and the hooks in them down like the flapping wings of a condor. The two meat hooks came together in midair like brain-crushing tongs with a sudden eruption of sparks as metal slammed against metal. But Stone was gone, having danced a good yard away. Scalzanni was fast, incredibly fast. He moved with the paranoid, darting speed of a fucking weasel. Stone studied the hooks in each of the Mafia don's hands. There was no opening for him, so he moved slowly but constantly backward, always in a circle to Scalzanni's right. Out of the corner of his eye he noted the torpedoes watching with bemused grins as they let their .45s dangle loosely in their hands. They had no doubt as to the outcome of this particular match. He'd have to wait for the little slime to make a mistake, if he ever did, and then move in on him. The man's fighting style was just too hard to penetrate.

But it was Stone who made the mistake. Thinking he was still within the area he had scanned with his eyes, he stepped backward and found himself toppling over as his ankle was caught by a root. Suddenly he was lying flat on his back, his knife by his side. As he grabbed for it, all hell broke loose.

Scalzanni, seeing his opportunity, charged forward, flailing away with both of the hooks like some sort of psychotic Captain Hook. The first hand missed, but the second, as he came right up to his fallen adversary, was coming in on target. As the meat hook in the Mafia killer's right hand descended like a question mark searching for blood toward Stone's skull, Stone tightened his eyes and prepared for the blow.

It never came. Out of the shadows behind the Harley, a shape hurtled like a ball shot out of a catapult. Excaliber. His jaw opened as he leapt and suddenly the teeth came into violent contact with Scalzanni's wrist, holding the hook that was descending on Martin Stone's brain tissue. The dog slammed its jaws shut with all of the two thousand pounds per square inch it could exert, enough to chew through iron. A man's skinny wrist was hardly any resistance at all. The hand, still holding the hook, suddenly shot free and spiraled off through the night air as if looking for something to kill.

Excaliber continued his trajectory past the two men, coming down about eight feet off in the dirt. He instinctively stayed low as he hit, knowing the firepower would be erupting soon.

Stone didn't waste a second, taking advantage of the dog's attack to leap to his own feet. Before Scalzanni had time to realize he had just lost his right hand and all that went with it, Stone was up, his hand grabbing around the left wrist holding the second hook. As the Mafia chief's head swung back, Stone ripped the hook in a circle up and into the slime's face. The point of the hook dug straight into Scalzanni's narrow mouth, and as Stone ripped it up, as if hauling a piece of meat, the curved metal hook tore up through the skull, then out the top.

It was as if Stone had the man impaled on an immense fishhook, and he quickly pushed his human "fish" backward. Scalzanni was in no position to resist, seeing as how his mouth, throat, and entire head were pierced clean through with his own weapon. His eyes twisted around madly in his head, which was already becoming coated with red that bubbled out the fracture at the top of the skull and from his nose and mouth. Making sure the frantically struggling Scalzanni was between him and the torpedoes, Stone rushed backward until he saw the black lake filled with arms and heads. With a burst of strength he gripped the handle of the meat hook and heaved with everything he had. The Mafia chief fairly took off from the ground and flew up into the air. He didn't come down until he had gone a good twenty feet out above the black, oily swamp of death—the swamp where he had ordered hundreds of others thrown without a thought as to their wretched screams.

Now he couldn't scream, a half-inch-thick piece of metal taking up the space where his vocal cords used to be. But he could flail around like a chicken with its head cut off, which he did. But only for a few seconds, for the swamp was like quicksand, like glue. And it pulled at him, wanted him to join it. With a final ghastly burp of bubbles, the Mafia don of dons was sucked beneath the surface until only one finger barely poked through the slime-coated surface. It was as if the sea of death, as vast and all-consuming as it was, could take only a portion of a man of such darkness and evil. It would take it days to fully digest his flesh in its foul, poison-dripping jaws.

But Stone didn't wait around to look at Scalzanni's final gurglings. Even as he released the sick load into the air, he threw himself to the ground and rolled three times to the side. Not a second too soon, for as they saw their boss head to sea, the torpedoes opened fire, blazing away with both .45s as fast as they could pull the triggers. But shooting is one thing—hitting another. Stone, who had come to one knee and crouched low in the darkness, could see them both easily silhouetted by the lights of the mall behind them. He sighted up first one, dead center of the Cro-Magnon face, and pulled the trigger, then shifted the Ruger a fraction of an inch and fired again. Elapsed time—.76 of a second.

Forty feet away, two faceless corpses toppled over dead before they hit the cold ground. Stone rose from the dirt and walked forward edgily, the Ruger held out in front of him ready to spit hellfire. But there was no need. Not for these two, anyway. They were already sinking into the ground. Slowly, of course. But then, the dead are very patient.

Chapter Twenty _____

The pitbull walked over to Stone, snorting up a storm and spitting out a spray of red as it tried to rid its mouth of the foul taste. The taste of Scalzanni. For the blood had spewed out the mafioso's severed wrist and covered the animal's face from the tip of its nose to its neck. The dog looked like some sort of Darwinian nightmare, the first *Canine redfacus* in the world.

"You look like shit," Stone said, bending down to make sure the blood was all from someone else, which, as he glanced around the dog's head and neck, he saw was the case. "But you saved my damn ass again, dog." The animal looked up and squinted at Stone through inscrutable almond-shaped eyes as if to say, "If you weren't always about to get your ass turned to grass, it wouldn't have to be Wonder Dog to the rescue."

"Yeah, well, keep it up"—Stone grinned from one corner of his mouth—" 'cause I need all the fucking help I can get." The thought of that hook coming down on him, the last second when Stone could virtually feel the pointed tip tearing through his brain, that image would live in his mind forever. As would the image of the dog ripping off Scalzanni's entire hand. Of such things are the pleasant memories of old age built.

"Come on," he said, walking toward the Harley. The pitbull, of course not realizing that he looked like a walking advertisement for the Save a Battered Dog Foundation, tromped along at Stone's heels, his tongue hanging out of his mouth like an old, stretched-out piece of rubber tire. This was ending up to be a good evening, the dog was starting to decide. Fighting got its blood going, even helped its digestion. Why, after all the fuss, the animal suddenly realized, it had even built up another appetite. It let out a sharp whine as it jumped back up on the cycle—just to let Stone know that after its puking bout and its aerobics, it was hungry. Its vomit-scented breath, which came in hot, panting bursts of air into Stone's face, was enough to get his own stomach gurgling like a goddamn broken pipe.

"Pal, my present to you for saving my ass," Stone grumbled, turning his face away and trying to suck in a deep breath of the cold night air, "is going to be some goddamn dog mouthwash." He started the Harley through the darkness, straight toward the mall. The shit clearly *had* hit the fan. People were running everywhere down the corridors. Bells, alarms, and sirens were going off all over the place. There was no point in playing tag with the bastards. Stone was going in. Straight in.

The bike roared out of the darkness surrounding the mall and slammed up onto one of the concrete walkways like a steel buffalo ready to do battle. The few pedestrians dived for cover, flying off in all directions like bowling pins trying to flee the ball. Bent over far forward on the Electraglide like a cross-country racer, the dog equally clamped down and low to the seat, they tore down one of the side corridors at a good forty miles per hour. It was all junk here—the windows for the first few blocks containing only hats, camouflage outfits, paintings of famous killers. But after he'd gone about a quarter of a mile, Stone saw the displays, which rushed by the bike in a blur, change to firearms. Rifles, SMGs, machine guns—all filled the windows.

He pressed a small button just below the trigger mounted in the right handlebar of the droning Harley and swiveled the muzzle of the .50-caliber machine on the front of the bike so it turned like a python to the right. Stone slammed his finger down on the trigger, and the steel barrel sprayed out a hailstorm of destruction. The slugs tore through the big windows, ripping them to shreds. Behind Stone, who was moving just fast enough not to get nicked by the debris, the mall walkway began exploding out from every window in a wall of twisting glass shrapnel. Those who were walking along the corridor were cut into bloody dolls that danced peculiar jigs and screamed incomprehensible songs before they collapsed into oozing twitching pieces of red meat on the cement sidewalk.

But Stone didn't stick around to see the end of the performance. He just wanted to be the cause. He tore toward the middle of the mall, to where he knew April was still being held—if the pre-death words of Scalzanni were true. And the bastard had had no reason to lie to Stone then, as he believed he was about to sink one of his hooks right into Stone's brain. Pity, things hadn't quite worked out. Stone kept his finger on the trigger of the .50-caliber, decimating whole blocks of windows filled with weapons. The screaming slugs kept going after they slammed through the glass— they ripped into things inside the stores, into ammo boxes, shells, boxes of powder. Explosions began taking out whole walls in the trail that Stone left behind him. Concrete ceilings erupted up into the air; chunks of car-sized walls spun lazily up a few hundred feet before slamming back down and into something or someone else. For those caught in the fire and concrete maelstrom, it was proof—if any was needed —that there *was* a hell on earth.

Then Stone saw her—blocks ahead—in the same glass prison that he had been gassed in. He came to a complete stop, took out his binocs, and sighted down the long corridor as clouds of smoke began rising behind him. He could see her—sweet April—so drugged out that her lips hung down like a Ubangi's, her eyes open enough to let only a pinprick of light into them. He couldn't see another living soul down the entire mall. Not one. Stone knew it was a trap. Knew that they were waiting for him. But then, he wasn't exactly planning things out on a drafting board these days.

"Come on, dog, the night is young," Stone said, reaching around and patting the pitbull, which was sniffing at the air with a concerned expression. It knew something big was in the offing. "We're going to go looking for some dog biscuits, okay?" Stone smirked at the dog, laughed, and sat down hard in the seat. All in all, the pitbull didn't like the way its master had just said whatever he'd said. Somehow he knew in his innate animal wisdom that dog biscuits were not on the agenda.

Stone revved the Harley and suddenly let its brakes go as if it were a jet plane gaining power for takeoff. The 1200-cc motorcycle shot forward like a Brahma bull coming out of the pen. For a few seconds the bike careened all over the wide mall corridor—some asshole had spilled a whole tray full of drinks hours earlier. The dog let out an earsplitting whine as the bike went all the way over at a forty-five-degree angle. But Stone slammed his boot down, kicked hard, and the bike evened out again.

Once upright, the Harley shot forward like a rocket. He had gone perhaps a third of the distance—two blocks—toward April when they opened up. *Opened up* was hardly the term for it, as instantaneously, all the stores on both sides of the mall erupted with automatic and semiautomatic gunfire. They had taken the girls out but left the windows, not wanting to give away the fact that anything was amiss. Shards of glass ripped toward Stone and Excaliber, peppering parts of them with tiny fragments of glass, and instantly they began to bleed. Stone swiveled the machine gun back and forth on the bike. This time he kept his finger on the trigger. Finger-sized slugs shot out of the smoking muzzle and migrated into the stores. Blood-soaked bodies came flying out of them, bouncing from wall to wall and then spitting right out in the street, corpses ready to return to the dirt.

Stone swiveled the machine gun constantly so the scythe of firepower reached into every store, ripping into the darkness from which scores of little flames kept erupting as they fired back. The gauntlet was almost overwhelming, and as he felt slugs whizzing through the air all around him, Stone knew that if he had the nine lives of cat—as someone had once suggested—he was about to use up about fifty of them.

But there was no turning back. Not with the only damn person he ever cared about on the whole fucking planet being kept prisoner inside a piece of Plexiglas. Stone got to within a block of the plastic jail cell when the level of fire got absolutely scalding. He wheeled into a doorway, emptying a blast inside the place and hearing a few satisfying screams from the darkness, then skidded around on one foot, bringing the bike to a squealing and dusty stop. The pitbull let out a groan of dismay, but it was so dizzy from the ride that it couldn't really muster up more than a low howl. Stone ripped out his Redhawk with the telescopic sight and ran to the shattered window frame, holding the big Magnum in his right hand and his Uzi autopistol in the other. If death was stalking him, it was going to have to take a bellyful of bullets in the process.

Stone barely reached the smashed frame when he saw two figures drawing a bead on him from across the street. He swung the Uzi up and pulled the trigger hard, turning the bucking auto from side to side fast. Two muscle-bound torpedoes, their bodies jerking around like someone had just put gerbils up their asses, blood pouring from numerous holes in their faces and chests, came exploding out of the window frame and into the walkway. They both seemed to walk forward a few steps, as if anxious to meet Martin Stone, the man who had just killed them. Then they both collapsed into the glass-strewn cement, falling atop each other like two drunken buddies who had just painted the town—and themselves—red.

Stone carefully tilted his head around the side of the blasted window and saw April—and his eyes widened in horror. They were undoing the lock, opening the door, taking her away. They weren't even going to let him get to the bait. He was a fool for thinking he had even the slimmest chance. Still, it wasn't over yet. He leaned around quickly, as slugs danced by him, looking for a fleshy partner. Stone lifted the big Ruger and stared through the floating red-dot sight atop it. He got the thugs back in the center of the dot just as the Mafia gunner was pulling April down onto the stone corridor. Stone pulled the trigger hard, and the torpedo turned and caught the slime in the right shoulder. The sheer force of the big .44 slug ripped into the abductor, and the man flew around like a top and slammed into the wall behind him.

But, lest Stone begin to feel hope, another one of the late Scalzanni's crew appeared from nowhere and grabbed April, who was starting to fall forward, not even able to stand up on her own, as drugged out as she was. Throwing her right over his shoulder, the mafioso ascended a ladder that led to the roof of a store. Stone kept his finger on the trigger of the Redhawk, following the bastard every step of the way, but there just wasn't a chance. A shot that would take him would just as likely kill or severly injure April. Bullets zeroed in on Stone as snipers in buildings up and down the mall were finding his range, but he kept watching, praying for a clear shot.

Suddenly things got even worse. For as the torpedo reached the roof and climbed out, a chopper appeared out of the dark, smoky mists that stroked the mall from every side. Before Stone's horrified eyes, the helicopter darted down onto the concrete roof. The mafioso threw his captive female roughly into the small cockpit, which was just big enough for two, then jumped in behind her, picking her up again and putting her on his knee. Stone could see him gesticulating wildly at the pilot, who took off frantically and with such speed that the chopper's spinning blade nearly collided with another three-story-high roof. Then he seemed to regain control and the craft beelined north—out of the burning city. Before Martin Stone could do a fucking thing about it, his sister was into the closing darkness, as if in the talons of a hawk heading off with its prey to some dank and foul nest.

"Fucking bastards," Stone screamed, knowing as he did so that his words were as useless as bullets in reaching the chopper. The storm of return fire was getting absolutely searing, reaching for him and drawing closer by the second. Stone pulled back inside, into the glass- and blood-splattered darkness, and jumped onto the Harley. The pitbull was attached to the seat like a piece of wallpaper to a wall, his head buried between his front paws, as if he just couldn't bear the sight of the carnage unfolding around him.

"Tough guy, huh?" Stone snorted as he jumped onto the seat in a flying leap. "Well, hang on, 'cause we're going to the rodeo." The dog would have howled back some sort of protest, but it didn't want to move its head even one inch into harm's way and so only was able to make a gurgling sort of sound from between its trembling paws. Stone leaned down far forward on the bike and pulled back hard on the throttle. The huge Electraglide shot forward like a stallion leaving the gate. It slammed through what had been the door frame of the place and skidded out into the firefight that was still blazing.

Without slowing, Stone curved the bike across the street and then straightened out, heading quickly back to the other side again, like a sailboat tacking back and forth. He shot up the block toward the Plexiglas cage where April had recently resided as shots pinged along the walls and concrete floors trying desperately to find some nice soft part of him.

Then Stone saw the bastard he had winged lying there, his eyes still open, breathing hard. He headed toward the man, who was half lying behind a concrete trough. Stone brought the Harley to a skidding stop, the tires coming to rest only a foot or so from the hit man, who, even in his pain, winced as he thought for a second that Stone was going to run him over.

"Where?" Stone screamed out, his right boot digging into the big stomach of the Mafia torpedo. "Where the fuck did they take her?" He lifted the Redhawk and slowly aimed it between the man's eyes. "You might actually live, asshole, though you won't look too pretty—if I *don't* kill you." He lowered the pistol to the slime's face until the wide black muzzle was about an inch from the tip of the bleeding nose. "Now tell me—where did they take her?"

"Sure—I'll—I'll tell you." The torpedo smirked. "Don't mean nothing to me. "To Alamosa. It was Vindigi's idea. He said he knew who would want the bitch. I don't know who—I swear. Alamosa—that's where. Alamosa . . ." Slugs were pouring down now, and Stone felt one shoot into the leather seat just between him and the dog. The animal let out a sound like a fingernail scraping along a chalkboard but didn't move an inch from its ostrichlike position.

"Now let me live! You promised, man, you," the hit man pleaded, his dry, thick lips sliding over each other in fear.

"I lied," Martin Stone said coldly, not feeling very generous today. He pulled the trigger and turned his head as the whole center of the man's face turned into some sort of Picasso painting. Then the corpse toppled over and would now have to make its pleas to the keeper of the thick gates of heaven.

Stone shot around and pulled back hard on the accelerator. The bike sat up in a wheelie for several seconds, giving a good target to the snipers a block or so behind him. A slug tore into the fatty part of his leg before the bike came down again, and he grunted with pain. This was crazy. He'd be ready for the strainer in a few more seconds. He saw a concrete-walled store to the left and suddenly veered toward it, firing a scissor of slugs back and forth, twice, right into it. Without stopping to give a business card, he drove the bike straight through the door, which fractured off its frame and flew off. He came to a skidding stop inside, ripping his eyes around to see if there was danger.

But the only danger was in slipping in the blood of the dead would-be assassin, his double-breasted suit riddled with smoking holes through which rivulets of red were running. Stone glanced behind him to make sure the pitbull wasn't going to run off chasing rats or something, but the animal was clutched solidly around the seat, its eyes shut as tight as bear traps. A wall of fire began reaching for the store he was in, and slugs zipped into the walls, richocheting off so that in seconds the large concrete-walled room was filled with ringing, whistling lead bugs just looking for a place to land.

His eyes caught a doorway in the back, a curtain hung over it. "Beggars can't be fucking choosers," Stone mumbled to himself as he twisted the handle of the Harley and it rocketed forward, straight into the curtain. For all he knew, there was a brick wall on the other side. Well, he was about to find out the experimental way. Stone involuntarily closed his eyes as the bike hit the black cloth drape. But when he opened them a split second later, they were in the back of another store that must have stood in the next corridor over. There were stacks of knives and blackjacks all over the place, but Stone just wheeled the Harley through the long room, knocking it all over and sending tables flying. The metal bull in a china shop whinnied and snorted like a thing alive, wreaking havoc throughout the place.

As Stone came roaring by, men jumped as if they were diving off the high board. To each side he saw the front door just ten yards ahead and aimed for it when out of the corner of his eye he saw the proprietor of the store, a fat, balding sludge of humanity, rise up from behind the cash register trying to sight Stone up in his 12-gauge double-barrel. Stone knew instantly that he didn't have time to swivel the .50-caliber around. Besides, the bastard was at the wrong angle; the gun would never reach him. Acting with lightning-quick reflexes, he ripped the bike to the right at the same second he twisted the throttle. The Harley moved so fast, it outran the speed of the fat man's finger. The 1200-cc hit a stack of blankets piled up in front of the counter and went up and off of them like a ramp. The front wheel of the bike slammed into the top part of the storekeeper's face and chest, cracking it all to pieces, slamming the skull into two almost symmetrical pieces, both of which fell off to the sides, the entire brain flopping down and onto the floor like an egg from out of its shell or some hideous jellyfish from the very bottom of the sea, trying to find a home.

The Harley rocketed over the corpse and straight into the front window where the front tire slammed through the display of cardboard figures—one guy taking another guy out with a blackjack. Then he was into the glass, which sprayed out as if they'd just gone through a waterfall of exploding chandeliers. When he dared open his eyes again after a few seconds to make sure none of the glass got in them, Stone saw that he had come completely through the block and was now on a new, undamaged mall corridor. And not a guard was anywhere.

This one was filled with women, naked, drugged out of their young, terrified minds. Stone couldn't let them stay on the inside—not with what he had in mind to do. He remembered seeing one of the goons who had just abducted April reaching down to the front of the Plexiglas booth she had been in.

Stone stopped the bike, jumped off, and searched at the base of the first of a whole long block of the glass cages. He found what looked like a control box and saw two instructions: Open Window-One, and Master Control—Open All Windows This Block." But there were just keyholes beneath the writing. And he didn't have the fucking keys.

"Shit," Stone spat in exasperation. What was he going to do, call out for a fucking locksmith? He reached for the .44 and ripped it out, holding the muzzle about six inches from the "Master" keyhole. He turned his head and fired. The bullet turned the whole cylinder into a mass of twisted brass, and every prison window down the corridor clicked open. Stone jumped back on the bike and rode slowly down the street, screaming at the prisoners to get out.

"This whole place is going up. You hear me, girls? Get the hell out of here. If you can move and the one in the next booth can't, help her." A few of them seemed to stir and push out against the windows, which swung open easily. But the rest either half dozed or looked at Stone like he was a rooster from Mars. He swiveled the .50-caliber so that it was aimed at the top of their booths and above their heads, and let loose with a burst. He fired down a line nearly a hundred feet long, so glass and wood and cement went flying all over the place. The explosion made a hell of a lot noise, which had been Stone's intention.

That seemed to wake most of them up, he noted with satisfaction as he kept on driving slowly. "Move—get the hell out of here. I'm telling you, this whole place is going to go up in one hour. You hear me? One hour. Get the fuck out of here." With Stone screaming and cursing commands, the pitbull joining in with a bloodcurdling howl and an occasional firing of the .50-caliber machine gun, the girls began stirring a little more. In fact, they positively hauled ass once they saw he was serious. Dozens of naked women began running like wild animals down all the mall corridors.

"Head to the woods," Stone yelled, turning from side to side. "Find clothes for yourselves, blankets, anything to keep warm. But get out fast. And don't look back. You're free. Free, goddamm it, free!" But like most imprisoned masses, the girls had not the slightest idea of how to be free. Terrified, their arms clasped around their melony and peachy breasts, they wished to be back in their drugged states of painlessness, back in their warm, temperature-controlled plastic worlds where everything was taken care of for them and they hardly existed. But their fear of Stone's screams; of his machine gun, which ripped down at their heels; and of the insane look on the demon dog behind him on the motor-cycle sent them fleeing for their very lives down the corridors of the mall of death.

Chapter Twenty-one _____

S tone spent the next fifty minutes riding up and down
the rows of stores, sending up the weapons he could
see in eruptions of exploding shells and rifles, shooting
off the master controls of the glass-encaged girls, freeing
them, sending them out into a cruel world—but still a
world. Better than being the slave whores they would have
become. It looked pretty crazy, hundreds of the naked, nu-
bile women racing through the smoke, through the crowds
of visitors to the mall who were all panicking now and stam-
peding down the walkways.

When, as far as he could ascertain, Stone had freed virtually all of the display women, he tore down one of the side
corridors, virtually unnoticed. In pure panic, a man can go
anywhere, do anything. His father had taught him that. And
it was true. The Mafia guards just ran around firing into the
air, not knowing who was responsible or what was going on.
And with Scalzanni gone, no one was even giving orders
anymore.

Stone took the bike up to fifty miles per hour as he shot
through the waves of smoke that now swept down every
street. The few psychotic-looking drunks he tore past, the
only residents of this more run-down part of the mall complex, reached out with gangrenous arms at Stone, as if trying
to take him down into hell with them. But the hands only
clawed at wisping air as the motorcycle ripped through them
in a blur of metal and the scent of gunpowder.

Within five minutes he was out of the mall completely. He pulled the bike to a stop at a rise about half a mile away and a hundred feet or so up. It was a little breastwork of sand and small rocks in the middle of nowhere from which to look down on the devastated mini-city below. Trickles of white and gray smoke rose from a hundred places, as numerous stores burned and explosions went off here and there. But it wasn't enough. Not by a long shot. They could still fix it up again—repair the damaged walls, put in new display windows, and soon be selling their wares of death, their sex slaves. Stone didn't like the idea at all.

He took out the field glasses and checked the hills to the northern side, then swept them back and forth along the long, smoky corridors of the mall. The girls were out—most of them, anyway. He could see them streaming along dirt roads, up the sides of hills to the north a mile or so. He undid the lever on the side of the Harley and swiveled out the launching tube of the 89-mm Luchaire missile system. He had loaded it at the bunker, ready for quick use. But now he had all the time in the world. He sighted on the large gas tank that sat atop a three-story warehouse in the center of the mall. The tank was a cylinder, immense, thick, perhaps sixty feet long by twenty high, that supplied all the fuel to the mall. One of the late Scalzanni's greatest prides.

Stone aimed up through the sighting system of the Luchaire until he figured he was just about dead-center on the thing. Then he raised it a foot for drop, as the target was about three-quarters of a mile off. He pulled the trigger, and the launching tube spat out a long tongue of orange and red as the entire bike shook from the backflow. The long missile emerged from the tube as if ready to go into orbit, and streaked through the cold night, leaving a trail of white behind it as its jet flame hurled it toward the gas tank. When it hit, just a few feet from where Stone had aimed, there was a flash that seemed to fill the entire sky, and he pulled his face away. The wall of hot air that swept across his body nearly pushed him down.

When he turned back a few seconds later, Stone could see the flat fireball that spread clear across the entire mall. It was like a bubble of fire, consuming everything in its grip, a dome of yellow. The entire contents of the tank were going up at once, consuming everything in a withering heat that would leave only ashes, indistinguishable from one another. The place was finished. That was for damn sure. The fireball of instant death was already rolling back a little, but it had set the entire complex aflame. There would be nothing, nothing left.

Stone hoped the innocent had gotten out. If there were such things anymore, he thought with a dark laugh. He still had the bitter taste of both the Mickey Finn that Peaches had drugged him with and the yellow gas from April's little den, all floating around the back of his throat. That—plus the dank, oily odor of burning chemicals and flesh that per-meated the moist air—made for quite a wretched mouthful. The night smelled like a corpse. But the stench was beyond him. For in his mind's eye all he could see was that line of hideous, mutated cripples, masked, pierced men, the wretched leftovers from Scalzanni's experiments in pain. He saw them walking, stumbling through the forest, holding one another up, leaving behind them a trail of blood a mile wide.

"Jesus Christ, God, somebody up there," Stone muttered, gritting his teeth hard as the night wind started coughing down curtains of cold, bitter air. "Help those poor bastards to die."

The pitbull sat up high on the bike. He watched the goings-on below with unfathomable brown eyes, sitting ab-solutely straight, his front feet pushing down in front of him so he formed an almost triangular symmetry with his body on the seat. He looked perfect. An object in harmony with himself. With a pose that had made even the earliest men revere and exalt his kind. For they were beyond understand-ing. Excaliber sat frozen, in perfect canine meditation, mus-ing on the murderous ways of man.

"Come on, dog," Stone said suddenly as the black, radio-active clouds started dropping down like avalanches from the sky. "We got to get the hell out of here." There was a deep rumbling from above, and it shook the ground beneath him in powerful subsonic waves that made his bones feel as if they were being tossed inside a blender. A drop of the black liquid hit his nose.

"Oh, fuck," Stone said, snarling at the dropping storm. As if he needed more trouble. "Dog, get your ass in astro-cruise position," Stone screamed as he pulled out the tarp from the emergency pack in the back. He sat down and wrapped the space blanket around both of them, tucking it under the dog's sides so it was completely covered, as was Stone, at least up to his shoulders and chest. He wrapped a piece of torn material around his mouth and started the bike forward just as a bolt of lightning arched over the entire mall and a wall of water tumbled down from the skies like the wrath of God, black and unstoppable, ten billion gallons of steaming atomic raindrops.

"We got to get to shelter before we get boiled like fucking lobsters, man. I mean, it's coming dog, it's coming down." Stone knew he probably sounded slightly hysterical, and the dog didn't like it at all, sending back a terrified howl as his part of the space blanket began shivering violently in stark fear. Stone released the clutch, and they shot down the back road, the Harley's tires spraying out a brown arch of dirt into the black air.